A Clockwork Christmas

Welcome to A Clockwork Christmas, a heartwarming holiday adventure set within the ever-expanding world of Jedidiah Davenport. Amid frost-covered prairies and flickering lamplight, invention and wonder meet the timeless spirit of Christmas, blending steampunk spectacle with the warmth of friendship, courage, and discovery.

Taking place between the events of Quest for the Lost Relic and The Mechanical Rebellion, this standalone tale bridges two eras of the Davenport saga—one chapter closing on mystery and exploration, the next poised to open on a world preparing for change. Here, we find Jedidiah and his companions not in battle or pursuit, but in a season of reflection that quickly turns into an unexpected test of ingenuity and heart.

When a daring holiday hold-up sparks a chain of events that threatens Windmire Junction, familiar faces return to face a new kind of challenge. The eccentric Professor Phineas B. Hargroves, and the steadfast Matthew Colton join Jedidiah in a story of clockwork intrigue, unexpected heroism, and laughter amid chaos. What begins as a simple celebration becomes a race against time—one where snow, steam, and spirit intertwine in equal measure.

A Clockwork Christmas captures the essence of the Davenport world while standing proudly on its own—a celebration of courage, compassion, and the unbreakable bonds of close friends. As an added bonus, you might even spot a few familiar faces from Steampunk Velvet making their own small but meaningful appearances.

So pour a cup of cocoa, settle in by the fire, and prepare to journey once more into a world where gears turn, airships soar, and Christmas itself gleams with the magic of invention.

Still covered in soot and coal dust,
Jedidiah Davenport and Matthew Colton
reluctantly pose beside the Mayor of
Windmire Junction, Silas T. Windmire.

A Clockwork Christmas

A Jedidiah Davenport Holiday Special

BY PAUL EDWARD TURNER

Contents

CHAPTER I

The Christmas Hold-up

A bitterly cold wind whipped through frost-covered branches as a weathered freight wagon creaked along the frozen road into Windmire Junction. Two horses trotted steadily, their breath misting in the brisk air. The wagon bed was stacked with wooden crates labeled "*GIFTS – MILFORD CREEK ORPHANAGE.*"

The driver—an older man with frost in his beard—gripped the reins with one gloved hand and reached for his coffee tin with the other.

"Should be in town by noon," he remarked, glancing over at the younger man sitting beside him.

"Can't get there fast enough for me," the latter replied, staring nervously into the woods. "It's too quiet out here. I don't like it."

"Relax," the driver grunted. "The only thing out here is wind and trees."

"Guess you're right." The skittish young man tried to change the subject. "You think it'll snow?"

"The paper hasn't predicted any. I think…"

Suddenly, a sharp whistle cut through the air, interrupting him. Then came the voice—clear, commanding, and unmistakably female.

"That's far enough, gentlemen. I'll be taking over from here!"

The wagon groaned to a halt as a single rider emerged from the trees ahead. A woman in a long brown duster, corseted vest, and a brown leather top hat adorned with a set of brass goggles. In her gloved hands, she firmly gripped two gleaming sidearms. There was no need to introduce herself. Her wanted posters had been plastered all over Kansas.

"Jumpin' Jehoshaphat," the older man said under his breath. "Ain't you..."

She cut him off by tipping her hat and replying with a slight chuckle. "The one and only."

Suddenly, the female bandit spotted the young man reaching for his rifle. Before he could lay a hand on it, one of her weapons discharged—a slug struck the side of the barrel and sent the rifle tumbling out of the wagon.

"I wouldn't try anything like that again," she warned.

"We're just carrying supplies to the orphanage," the younger man said, hands raised. "A few toys,

A single rider emerged from the trees.
A woman in a long brown duster, corseted vest,
and a brown leather top hat adorned with
a set of brass goggles.

that's all. Along with some blankets, books, fruitcake..."

"Fruitcake?" she chuckled. "Now that's worse than any crime I've ever committed!"

In one quick motion, the bold outlaw swung down from her horse and approached the wagon. After ordering the two men to step aside, she instructed the younger one to tie her horse to the back of the wagon. While he did this, she picked up his weapon, emptied it, and leaned it against a tree.

"What in tarnation did you do that for?" the older man asked, confused.

"Just so you don't get any ideas while I'm riding away." With that, she climbed onto the buckboard and looked back at them.

"Do me a favor," she said, resting one pistol on her thigh while holstering the other.

The two men looked at each other, then back at her. They both realized they didn't have much choice in the matter.

"Tell Mayor Windmire… *Two-Gun Kate* says Merry Christmas!"

With that, she holstered her pistol, slapped the reins, and vanished down the road.

****

The next day, December 19th, 1881, about ninety miles southeast of where the two freight drivers had stood dejected by the side of the road, Davenport Ranch was overflowing with the holiday spirit.

"*Deck the hall with boughs of holly, fa la la la la la la la la!*" Three men sang in perfect harmony as they marched down a hillside toward a stately Victorian manor.

Jedidiah Davenport led the way, gripping the top of an eight-foot cedar tree. On the opposite end, carrying the heaviest portion, was his best friend and childhood companion, Matthew Colton. Walking between them, and towering over them both, was Professor Phineas B. Hargroves.

Each man was dressed in festive winter attire. Jedidiah and Matthew wore Christmas-colored variations of their usual caps—Jed's a deep red, Matthew's forest green—each still adorned with the brass-rimmed goggles that typically rested on the brims. Phineas, by contrast, wore a tall red top hat with a green band—eccentric and bold, perfectly in line with his theatrical personality.

All three wore thick red scarves, but Phineas' stood out with wide green diagonal stripes that matched the band of his hat.

They had just come from a nearby cedar grove that Jedidiah had planted ten years earlier on land his family had owned long before it was expanded into the now-famous Davenport Ranch, a spread of more than ten thousand acres running over a thousand head of cattle.

"*'Tis the season to be jolly,*" they continued to sing.

"*Fa la la la la la la la la!*" A bearded, rotund man suddenly stepped out onto the porch and began singing very loudly and very much off-key.

Jedidiah, Phineas, and Matthew all stopped in their tracks and looked over at him, trying not to burst into laughter.

"What's the matter, fellows?" the portly man asked, confused. "Why'd you stop singing? I thought we sounded great!"

"That was the problem..." Jedidiah thought quickly on his feet. "Pat, you sounded so good, you put the three of us to shame!"

Pat Bennington studied on this for a moment and then said, "Yeah, I guess you're right. Don't want to embarrass anybody." Suddenly, he snapped his fingers as a thought struck him. "Say, maybe instead of joining in with everyone at the big shindig, I should just sing a few numbers by myself."

Just the thought nearly made them lose their grip on the tree.

"Egads!" Phineas gasped.

"The idea kinda gets you, don't it, Hargy?" Pat chuckled. "Right here..." He motioned toward his own chest.

"It does have a similar feeling to heartburn,"

Phineas muttered under his breath.

"What was that?" Pat asked, not understanding what he had just said.

Jed spoke up before the professor could reply, "Uh, Pat, I don't think you'll have time. You'll be too busy keeping everybody fed with that amazing Christmas feast you're preparing!"

"Oh yeah, I forgot." Pat Bennington leaned back and tugged at his suspenders. "Everybody will be counting on me!"

"Hey, Jed..." Matthew suddenly spoke up from the rear. "Can we talk about this later and get this tree inside? It's getting heavy!"

Davenport quickly agreed. "It is unusually heavy considering three of us are carrying it."

"Three?" Pat suddenly burst into laughter. "From where I stand, only two of you are toting that load. One of you is just strutting along, lookin' all fancy."

Jedidiah immediately whirled around while Matthew peeked through the branches. They both laid eyes on Phineas B. Hargroves, who didn't have one single gloved hand on the tree.

"I've been guiding you both!" he stated, as though it were ridiculous that he should even have to defend himself.

Jedidiah Davenport and Matthew Colton each groaned as they dropped the tree onto the ground.

"Land O'Goshen!" The rotund man suddenly

exclaimed. "I just realized we already have a perfectly good six-footer sittin' in the parlor."

"I know." Jedidiah nodded.

"Then why'd you cut down an eight-foot tree?" Pat asked, confused.

"This one isn't going in the house," Jed explained.

Pat furrowed his brow. "Then where's it goin'? You plannin' to put it on the deck of one of your airships?"

Matthew snorted. Phineas gave a theatrical gasp. "Don't give him any ideas."

"On the deck..." Jed grinned, already planning a third trip to the cedar grove in his head. "No. I've decided we're moving the Christmas party out to the barn this year."

"Well, that makes sense..." Pat turned and started to go back into the house, then suddenly started to look a little panicked. "The barn! Why in blazes would you..."

"Because we're not just hosting friends and a few townsfolk this year," Jed said. "We've got the entire Milford Creek Orphanage coming. The parlor's not gonna be big enough."

Pat blinked. "You don't want to have a Christmas party in a musty old barn!"

"It won't be musty when we get through with it." Jedidiah smiled. "We'll lay down some fresh hay, get some lanterns strung up, and I figured this tree would look mighty fine in the middle of it, surrounded by all my old furniture Phineas threw out."

"Your old furniture..." Pat gulped nervously.

"You remember," Jedidiah explained. "A few months ago, when the Professor bought all that new stuff and redecorated half of the house?"

"I vaguely recall something about that..."

"Well, at first I was furious when I found out he had my old stuff stored in the barn, but now I think it's going to work out just right for this event."

"What's the matter with you, Pat?" Matthew suddenly spoke up. "You look like you don't feel so well."

"Egads!" Phineas added. "My dear man, you do look rather pale."

"I think I'm gonna be sick..." The rotund man placed both hands on his ample stomach.

"Well, lie down and get some rest," Jed remarked as he bent down to pick up his end of the tree back up. "Come on, everyone." He glanced up at Professor Hargroves. "And I do mean everyone! Let's get this thing out to the barn."

"Barn!" Pat Bennington practically shouted. "Jed! Wait!"

"What is it now?" the young entrepreneur asked as he turned loose of the tree.

"What now... what now..." The rotund man thought hard for a moment before he quickly said,

"I want you to come inside and inspect the staff!"

"Staff? You mean you and Agatha?" Matthew chuckled, setting his end of the tree back down.

"He's referring to Cogsworth, Artemis, and Apollo." Phineas reminded him of the three automatons inside the house. Cogsworth was their permanent mechanical resident, while Artemis and Apollo were both being loaned to them by their good friend Jonathan Blake.

"Why do I need to inspect them?" Jedidiah asked impatiently.

"Well, I'm afraid they'll start acting all crazy again like that first mechanical monstrosity did when it came here and tried to deep-fry me with my own spatula!"

"That was a couple of months ago," Davenport huffed. "He hasn't shown any new signs of malfunctioning since, has he?"

"Well, no..."

Jed started to pick the tree up again, but quickly let it go as Pat added, "But you never know when it or one of the other two might start!"

"I give up!" Jedidiah sighed. "Let's go inspect the troops."

Once inside the stately Victorian manor, they found matronly housekeeper Agatha Porter supervising the small group of automatons, each outfitted with festive adornments.

Apollo carried a tray of steaming apple cider,

while Artemis wore a garland like a sash. The third one, known as Cogsworth, was toting a massive wreath he had been ordered to hang above the barn doors.

The mechanical man paused and stepped aside, allowing the humans to enter.

"Try placing that wreath over your shoulders," Phineas motioned for him to wear it like a giant necklace. "There. Now you resemble a festive gargoyle." He laughed heartily as he poked Matthew in the ribs with his elbow.

"What do you think, Jed?" Pat asked nervously, wringing his hands. He turned to the Professor. "Hargy, do they seem… normal?"

Phineas shrugged as he finished laughing. "All three appear to be operating within normal parameters."

"They look fine to me, too," Jedidiah added, slightly irritated. "Now, if nobody has any more objections, let's get that tree out to the barn."

"Wait!" Pat quickly stepped in front of the doorway. "Hold on! I just had a thought. Why don't we have Artemis and Apollo carry it?"

Jed squinted. "The tree?"

"Sure!" Pat beamed. "Would save you the trouble. I mean, look at it—big, awkward, heavy. Perfect job for a couple of strong metal men!"

"I'm not forcing the automatons to carry our Christmas tree," Jedidiah said. "It doesn't seem right, somehow."

"Why not, Jed?" Matthew spoke up. "It's awfully heavy for just the two of us."

Phineas adjusted his scarf. "Technically, they were built to handle much more strenuous tasks. This would hardly be a strain for them."

"It's not about what they can and can't handle. It's about tradition. It's about the holiday spirit. It's about..."

"Potential hernias?" Matthew groaned.

"Fine!" Jed huffed in defeat. "They can carry the tree, but we're decorating it and I'm putting the star on!"

"Now you're talking sense!" Agatha Porter finally spoke up. "Now, where is this tree you've been carrying on about, and where is it going?"

They told her it was just outside and needed to be placed in the center of the barn.

"You heard Jed!" Agatha snapped her fingers at Apollo and Artemis. "Go get that cedar and follow Cogsworth to the barn!"

Just as the last automaton had left the room, Jed turned to follow.

"Wait, wait, wait!" Pat yelped, blocking him again. "Why don't you sit down and enjoy some cider? I can go out there and supervise those three."

"Why would I do that?" Jed asked, brow raised.

"Well, you got your fancy new clothes on, and I know it's chilly out there, and a little icy. You know those boots you got on ain't got good traction. What if you slip and break something with the party less than a week away?"

Jed crossed his arms. "Pat, what is going on?"

"Nothing!" The rotund man said quickly. "Just... trying to keep you safe and warm and not horrified... I mean, not inconvenienced by anything in the barn."

Jed narrowed his eyes. "What exactly is in the barn?"

"Nothing!" The older man repeated, louder. "Just hay and walls and uh... barn stuff!"

Jed sighed. "Pat."

Phineas leaned toward Matthew and whispered, "He's hiding something."

"Obviously," Matthew whispered back.

Trying a different method, Pat Bennington chose to rely on Professor Phineas B. Hargroves' ego.

"Hey, Hargy," Pat continued to firmly stand in the doorway. "How's about showing us how that new contraption of yours works?"

"My dear man, we simply don't have time for such..." Hargroves started to protest, but the rotund man desperately cut him off.

"I'm really interested in seeing how a genius like you comes up with all these brilliant ideas."

Phineas started once more to argue, but then immediately changed his mind. "Genius, you say?

You really think I'm a genius?"

"Not just me, but everybody says it!"

"That's very true, they do!" The professor immediately agreed. "Well, in that case, which one would you like me to show you?"

"The one you've been working on in secret up in your room," Pat smiled. "The one you took back from the train robbery a couple of months ago."

"Pat!" Jedidiah exclaimed. "We don't have time for this!"

"I beg to differ, my dear boy," Phineas turned and started into the hallway. "There's always time for creative genius!"

"Fine! The two of you stay here and discuss your brilliance. Matthew and I are going to the barn!" Jedidiah brushed past Pat, who scrambled again to stop him but missed.

"Wait, Jed!"

"No," Davenport replied. "I've got to see how much work there is to do if this party's going to be ready by the end of the week."

"Jed, wait! I just remembered the hinges on the barn doors squeak—maybe I should oil them first!"

Too late. Jedidiah reached the massive double doors, grabbed the handles, and swung them open wide.

For a brief second, nothing was said.

Then—

"*AAAAAAHHHHH!*"

CHAPTER II

Meeting Mayor Windmire

"Jed!" Matthew shouted, sprinting toward the barn.

Pat froze at the doorway, visibly cringing. "Oh dear..."

Inside the house, halfway up the staircase, Professor Phineas B. Hargroves somehow managed to hear the screams. He rushed to his room, on the second floor, and peeked out the window. Once he realized that everyone was okay, he shrugged and picked up his newest invention.

By the time Matthew reached the barn entrance, Jedidiah had stumbled back a few paces, his hands on his head.

"What is it? What's wrong, Jed?" Matthew asked.

Davenport pointed a trembling finger inside the building. "Look for yourself!"

Matthew stepped in cautiously—then froze.

The barn was a disaster.

All of Jed's furniture, which he had won a few years ago at the county fair, had been destroyed. Cushions were shredded. Wooden legs splintered and scratched beyond repair. Feathers hung out in bunches. The fabric on one of the chairs appeared to have been ripped completely in half.

Phineas arrived a moment later, muttering boastfully about how his intelligence was beyond even his own comprehension. He stopped short, eyes widening. "Egads... it looks like a buffalo rampaged through an upholstery shop."

Jedidiah turned slowly toward Pat Bennington, who was still hovering nervously in the doorway. "Care to explain?"

"Sure," he smiled. "You just pick a subject and I'll do my best."

"How... why..." Davenport was far beyond upset and couldn't come up with words to express his frustration.

"Well, you see, Jed." Before Pat could stammer out an explanation, a sudden noise came from under the settee. All four men turned toward it.

From the shadows, a small pair of golden eyes peered out. A little black cat known as Panther stretched and came into view. He walked over and began rubbing his face against Jedidiah's pant leg. Then came the unmistakable sound of purring.

Glancing back at Pat, Jed suddenly caught the

connection and asked, "You mean to tell me this one little cat caused all this destruction?"

"Well, to tell you the truth, he might have had a little help..."

He cut his sentence short as he glanced up and spotted a second little cat climbing up on the back of an armchair. Her name was Dottie. She was Panther's older sister. She was smaller and rounder than he was, with a bobbed tail and a white patch of fur on her chest. She watched as Jed stooped down to pick up Panther. While he was bent over, Dottie gave in to temptation.

"NO!!!" Pat shouted just as she leapt into the air and landed with a thud on Jed's back. Her claws pierced all layers of his clothes.

Jedidiah immediately screamed both in pain and in utter shock.

Pat Bennington rushed over, picked Dottie up, and dusted off Jedidiah's coat. "No harm done!" he announced, "She didn't even pull a single thread out of place."

The young entrepreneur stood straight and took a beat to compose himself. He turned to look at Dottie, who had just been placed on the seat of the armchair. Panther raced over and hopped up beside her.

"Pat, are you trying to say my furniture was destroyed by two little cats?"

"Well, no." He chuckled. "I was actually trying

hard not to say it!"

"How..." Jed's question was suddenly cut short as Agatha Porter came rushing into the barn, waving a telegraph that had just come off one of the ranch's private machines.

"Jed, one of your freight wagons with supplies for the Milford Creek Orphanage has been held up!" She waved the telegraph in the air. "Mayor Windmire wants you to come there personally and address the matter!"

"Gosh!" Matthew Colton exclaimed.

"Are you sure?" Jedidiah asked in disbelief.

"Read the rest of it for yourself!" Agatha started to pass it off to him, but it was intercepted by Phineas B. Hargroves, who gave it a quick glance.

"Madam!" he declared. "You already have!"

"Never mind!" Jed huffed as he snatched it from the older man's grasp. He began to read it over for himself.

Realizing how important the delivery was to the orphans, Davenport knew he had very little choice in the matter.

"Matt," he turned to his childhood friend, "prepare the Swift. We're going to Windmire Junction!"

"What about this mess?" Phineas asked with a flourish of one hand while he balanced his invention with the other.

Jedidiah sighed and asked him to stay behind

and oversee the preparations for the party. "Hire someone to reupholster and repair everything."

"Repair this stuff?" Hargroves looked around like he was being asked to do the impossible.

"Fine." Jedidiah Davenport huffed. "Order some new stuff!"

Phineas' eyes lit up for a moment. "New?"

"Simple basic... nothing extravagant!"

"In other words... cheap." Phineas frowned.

****

Soon after, engines thrummed to life as the Swift rose through the open roof of its hangar. Steam vented in thick plumes against the cold December air. The polished brass on the wooden hull gleamed in the sunlight as the airship climbed higher, banking northeastward toward Windmire Junction.

Below, Davenport Ranch spread out like a patchwork of frosted fields and timber lines. Along the lower acreage, numerous oil wells dotted the earth, derricks hunched like iron sentinels against the winter light. But it was the highest ridge that drew the eye—a newly constructed metal tower rising above the ranch, its latticework glinting like new brass. At its peak, signal vanes and copper filaments gleamed, a crown jewel for the wireless communication system Jedidiah and the others had pioneered during the Sky Race.

About two hours later, at approximately 1:30 PM on the afternoon of December 19th, 1881, the Swift descended toward the sprawling rail yards of Windmire Junction. Steam hissed from the airship's release valves as it touched down in the designated landing field beside the depot.

Two men in neatly pressed suits and derby hats were already waiting, their overcoats buttoned tight against the winter air. One stepped forward and tipped his hat.

"Mr. Davenport? I'm Thomas Avery, assistant to Mayor Silas T. Windmire. This is my colleague, Mr. Pierce. We're here to escort you and Mr. Colton to the mayor's office."

Jedidiah and Matthew followed the men through the bustling streets. The thriving town's brick storefronts and iron lampposts stood in sharp contrast to the crisp winter air, while the faint clang of a horse-drawn trolley's bell rang out in the distance.

By the time they reached City Hall, word had spread of their arrival. A cluster of newspaper reporters stood just inside the marble-floored lobby, cameras at the ready, notebooks in hand.

The mayor's office doors swung open, revealing Mayor Silas T. Windmire himself—a tall man with salt-and-pepper hair and a freshly waxed handlebar mustache. He stepped forward with a warm smile and both hands extended, his eyes radiating sincerity.

"Mr. Davenport, Mr. Colton—welcome to Windmire Junction. I only wish your visit were under better circumstances."

Jedidiah shook his hand. "I understand one of my freight wagons was ambushed?"

Windmire's expression darkened with concern. "Yes. A most grievous affair for the Milford Creek Orphanage, was it not? Despicable... utterly despicable." He glanced at the reporters, then back at Jedidiah. "Two-Gun Kate and her gang will not get away with this. I swear to you—justice will be served."

"So you know who held up the freight wagon?" Jedidiah turned to the Mayor, slightly confused. This wasn't in the telegram he'd received earlier.

"Of course," Windmire chuckled. "Same dastardly outlaw that's been attacking our fair city for weeks now!"

One reporter stepped forward. "Mayor Windmire, is it true the gang made off with the entire wagon?"

"I'll be making a full statement later this afternoon," Windmire replied, his tone firm yet measured. "For now, my priority is working with Mr. Davenport to see that those orphans still receive a proper Christmas and aren't turned out into the streets."

Both Jedidiah Davenport and Matthew Colton turned and looked puzzled at the mayor over that last comment.

"Mayor Windmire!" Another reporter from the back spoke out. "Is it true that the freight wagon was carrying a lockbox filled with monetary donations for the orphanage?"

"Absolutely not, we don't ship large amounts of money..." Jedidiah tried to answer, but was immediately cut off by Silas T. Windmire.

"Yes," he said, slightly reluctantly. "I'm afraid it's true. All the money raised to help pay off the mortgage for the orphanage was in that shipment."

Outraged, Jedidiah Davenport whirled to look at the mayor. "What do you mean there was money aboard that wagon?"

"Obviously, it wasn't advertised," the politician replied reluctantly. "The fewer people who knew, the better."

"Including my company?" The owner of the Davenport Dispatch & Delivery company turned to his childhood friend, who was also his second in command. "Did you know anything about this?"

"Of course not, Jed!" Matthew Colton scoffed. "I would never approve anything like that."

Seeing how quickly the reporters were jotting everything down, the Mayor promptly tried to de-escalate the situation to avoid any bad publicity.

"Gentlemen, please," he said with a calming

gesture toward the press. "We will recover from this. In fact, I have already begun arranging a benefit dinner this Wednesday evening. The proceeds will go toward replacing the lost donations in full, and perhaps even improve upon them."

He turned to Jedidiah and Matthew, his expression earnest. "I would be honored if you both would remain in Windmire Junction as my guests —and attend the event. Your presence would mean a great deal to the community, especially to the children of the orphanage."

"That's very kind of you," Jedidiah replied cautiously, still unsettled by the news of the money.

"Kindness," Windmire said with a warm smile, "is the least we can offer one another in these troubling times. Now, if you'll turn toward the camera, I believe the photographers wish to capture a few images for tomorrow's papers. A show of unity will go a long way toward lifting the town's spirits."

"But we really can't stay." Jed was trying to speak above the noise of the reporters and the hiss of flash powder. "We need to get back to the ranch and prepare for the Christmas party on the 24th."

"Nonsense!" The mayor kept smiling for the cameras. "You'll stay here as my guests. I insist!"

As Windmire finished speaking, the deep chime of the grandfather clock in the corner of his office rolled through the room, each note echoing off the walls.

Jedidiah automatically reached for his pocket watch, but the mayor raised a hand with a faint smile.

"No need, Mr. Davenport," he said. "That clock is serviced weekly and keeps perfect time. You can set your watch by it."

Jedidiah nodded and slipped the ornate object back into his vest.

"Now, gentlemen, I say again, turn toward the camera." Windmire smiled.

After several photos had been taken, Windmire clapped his hands together, drawing the attention of everyone in the room.

"Now, before you scatter to file your stories, let me offer some friendly advice," he said warmly. "If you wish to attend Wednesday's benefit dinner, I suggest you secure your places now. I've invited members of the press from all over our great nation to cover this gala, and I expect every seat in the hall to be filled. It will be an evening to remember —for the children, for the orphanage, and for the spirit of Windmire Junction itself."

The reporters murmured among themselves, several scribbling notes and glancing at each other as though already calculating how soon they could reserve a spot.

Following a subtle nod from the mayor, Thomas

Avery and Mr. Pierce stepped forward.

"That's all for now," Avery announced, raising his voice above the hum of conversation. "No more questions at this time."

The two men began guiding the reporters and photographers toward the exit, politely but firmly ushering them out into the lobby. The rustle of notepads faded as the doors closed behind them.

Windmire exhaled slowly, his warm smile softening into something more measured. He gestured toward the chairs in front of his desk. He eased himself back into his own seat, angling slightly to the side. One arm draped casually over the chair's armrest while the other rested on the desk, fingers tapping in a slow, deliberate rhythm.

"Please, gentlemen, sit. We can speak freely now."

"I meant every word I said out there," the mayor continued, lowering his voice. "The children of the Milford Creek Orphanage are counting on us. I intend for this benefit dinner to not only replace what was lost, but to remind our town of the strength we share in times of hardship."

Matthew folded his arms. "I just wish we'd been told about the money."

Windmire gave a slow, sympathetic nod. "Understandable. I kept that detail from nearly everyone—too many ears in this city are bent toward the wrong people."

Mayor Windmire sat with one arm draped
casually over the chair's armrest while the other
rested on the desk, fingers tapping in a slow,
deliberate rhythm.

"Then how do you think the press found out about it?" Jedidiah leaned forward. "Do you think someone on the inside tipped them off?"

"Perhaps," Windmire said carefully, as he continued to tap on the desk. "But let's leave speculation for another time. For now, the best thing we can do is make sure Wednesday's dinner is a success."

Jedidiah leaned back in his chair, shaking his head. "I'm sorry, Mayor, but we need to return to Spoon Fork. There's a great deal of preparation to be done before our Christmas party."

Windmire stopped tapping his fingers for the first time. "Mr. Davenport," he said evenly, "I cannot overstate the importance of this benefit. The children are relying on us. And while the dinner is two days away, your presence here in the days leading up to it will inspire confidence in the townsfolk and encourage larger donations."

Jedidiah's jaw tightened. "I understand, but there's no reason we can't come back."

Windmire gave a slow, measured nod, as though weighing the cost of pushing further. Finally, he smiled again, though it didn't quite reach his eyes. "Very well. But I trust you will keep your word."

"I've never broken it yet," Jed said firmly.

A few minutes later, they stepped back into the cold winter air. Steam from the depot chimneys drifted overhead as they made their way.

Matthew reached into his coat pocket, unwrapped a neat little rectangle, and broke off a square. "Want a piece?" he offered.

Jed glanced down, recognizing the wrapper immediately—cream-filled chocolate, imported from England. "Where'd you get that?"

"Brought it from home," Matthew said around a mouthful. "Figured I might need a snack."

A small smile tugged at Jed's mouth. "You know... We've still got a few cases of that back at the ranch. We could give them out to the children."

Matthew grinned. "Now that's the Christmas spirit."

The two men climbed aboard the airship, the hum of its engines rising as the Swift prepared to lift off. Matthew leaned over the railing to make sure the mooring lines were released.

Jedidiah moved toward the control levers. "We'll be home in no..." His sentence was suddenly cut short.

A deafening crack split the winter air. The deck lurched violently beneath their feet as a blast erupted from below, where the Swift's boiler sat just forward of the keel. A burst of white steam and black smoke billowed up through the grates, carrying with it the sharp tang of scorched metal.

Matthew staggered backward, lost his footing, and toppled over the railing. Jedidiah was thrown forward, slamming into the base of the helm.

CHAPTER III

Patent Pending Disaster

Moments after the explosion, Jedidiah Davenport staggered to his feet. Smoke rolled across the deck in thick gray billows, stinging his eyes and burning his throat. The acrid tang of scorched metal filled the air.

"Matt!" he shouted, coughing hard. "You alright?"

"I got tossed for a loop." From somewhere beyond the port side railing came Matthew Colton's voice. "But I'm hanging on."

"Yeah, that explosion was rough. I got banged up pretty bad myself." Jed reached up, removed his cap and goggles, and ran his fingers through his hair. He staggered over to the railing, and that's when he noticed two sets of knuckles gripping it tight. He leaned over and spotted his longtime friend clinging to the side of the ship.

"Matt!" He shouted, finally realizing that when

his friend said he was hanging on, he meant it literally. Jedidiah grabbed Matt's wrists and began to pull him over the side.

Below them, shouts were already rising from the rail yard. Dozens of townsfolk craned their necks toward the airship, pointing at the column of smoke curling skyward.

Once Matthew was back on the deck, Jedidiah raced over to a supply closet. He yanked the door open, revealing a brass-and-copper portable fire extinguisher. It was one Phineas had designed and equipped every airship with. Without hesitation, he swung the leather harness over his shoulders, tightened the straps, and lowered his goggles.

Steam hissed faintly from the pressure valves as he gripped the coiled hose, thumb resting on the lever. "Hang on," he muttered to the Swift before disappearing below deck.

Heat surged up the narrow stairwell, the flicker of orange flames casting wild shadows across the walls. Jed planted his feet, aimed the nozzle, and pulled the lever. A powerful jet of hissing chemical foam blasted forward, smothering the fire in thick, white layers.

Minutes later, Jedidiah emerged from the hatch, unstrapping the extinguisher harness and setting it against the wall. His face was streaked with soot, his shirt damp with sweat.

"The fire's out," he said, catching his breath,

"but the boiler's beyond repair. We're not taking off until it's replaced."

Matthew's brow furrowed. "How long will that take?"

"A couple of days at least," Jed replied. "We'll need to take the old one completely out in order to put a new one in. We have a few extra ones back at the ranch. We'll have Phineas bring one here aboard the Icarus. In the meantime..." He glanced over the rail at the growing crowd. "We'd better find a hotel and a telegraph office."

Jed and Matthew left the Swift in the care of a few local men they generously paid to keep an eye on things until they returned. After this, they made their way through the throng of curious onlookers. A few more reporters tried to press them for questions, but they declined to respond.

By the time the two reached the telegraph office, the streets were bustling with afternoon traffic. Wagons rattled past, their wheels crunching over the frost-covered ground, while shopkeepers swept their steps clear of dirt and grit. Evergreen garlands, tied with bright red ribbons, hung over doorways, and hand-painted wooden signs in the windows advertised holiday wares—peppermint sticks in tall jars, parcels of candied fruit, and bolts of rich fabric for Christmas gowns. The scent of fresh bread mingled with the sharper tang of roasted chestnuts from a street vendor's cart.

Families in their Sunday best strolled along the boardwalk, the ladies in fur-trimmed cloaks and feathered hats, the gentlemen in dark wool overcoats with polished brass buttons.

Jed stepped inside the telegraph office and scrawled out a brief but urgent wire to Phineas, explaining the damage and the need for a replacement boiler. He also included a message to Pat, asking him to send along however many cases of imported chocolate they had left.

****

Meanwhile, slightly over ninety miles southeast of Windmire Junction, a pale winter sun slanted through the open hay loft of the Davenport barn, catching in the drifting motes of dust. The scent of oiled wood and machine grease hung in the air. At the far end, Phineas B. Hargroves sat on an upturned crate with a thick mail-order catalog spread across his knees, a pencil tucked behind one ear. On a torn-up settee a few feet away, two little black cats, Panther and Dottie, lay curled up asleep.

Every few moments, Phineas would pause to circle an illustration of a parlor chair, a table, or a sideboard—pieces he deemed worthy of replacing the tattered furniture in the barn.

Beside him sat his latest invention. It was housed in a wooden encasement no bigger than a large breadbox, compact enough to ride in a burlap sack and rest on his lap. A lattice of polished brass plates framed the boxy body, its edges bound with tiny rivets that gleamed in the loft's light. Copper piping coiled in graceful loops along the sides, feeding into a small, round boiler chamber fitted with delicate gauges and needle-thin valves that quivered faintly with each tick. From the top rose a short chimney, its rim crowned with a basic weathervane, turning slowly with a faint metallic whisper. A muted hum resonated within, as if the little machine were thinking to itself, its purpose known only to Phineas.

He leaned back, admiring his handiwork, and allowed himself a small, satisfied smile. In just a few days, the Davenport Ranch would host its annual Christmas gathering—and this year, he intended to make it unforgettable. The machine, if all went according to plan, would coax snow from the Kansas sky, ensuring a white Christmas that would surely delight one and all.

For now, though, he turned another page in the catalog, muttering, "Yes… that settee will do nicely. When Pat brings my tea, I'll have him wire this list to the company for immediate delivery." He was completely unaware that a telegraph was already making its way along the lines.

Suddenly, a sharp rap echoed from the barn door, drawing Phineas' attention from the page. He pushed himself up from the crate, brushing straw from his trousers, as the door swung open, revealing Pat Bennington standing there with a serving tray and a steaming cup of herbal tea.

"Snack time, Hargy," Pat said, stepping inside and setting the tray on the crate.

Phineas arched a brow. "Did you remember the biscuits?"

"Biscuits?" Pat looked confused for a moment. "Didn't bring no biscuits. Wasn't any left over from this morning, but I did bring you those fancy cookies you like so much."

"My dear man, those are..." Phineas shrugged and chose not to argue. "Thank you for remembering my *fancy cookies*."

Pat nodded as he glanced toward the odd little machine. "I'd ask you what that contraption does, but I've got a feelin' you'd tell me I wouldn't understand."

Phineas allowed himself a sly smile. "On the contrary, this device is so simple that even someone of your limited intellect could comprehend the intention of its design."

Pat hesitated. "Is that a compliment?"

Professor Hargroves nearly choked on the tea he was sipping over the thought of complimenting the individual in front of him. "Please, Patrick, don't make me laugh!"

"Somebody tell a joke?" He looked around the

room and settled his eyes on Panther and Dottie. Dottie merely rolled over on his side, her legs sticking up in the air because of how round her stomach was. Panther yawned, stretched, and turned his back to them as well.

"Why are you looking at those felines?" Phineas asked, irritated. "I thought you wanted to know about my latest invention!"

"Don't get your feathers ruffled, Hargy." Pat Bennington laughed. "I'm ready to hear all about your newest creation. What is it?"

"It's a weather machine."

"Do you call it that because you don't know whether or not it will work?" The rotund man chuckled.

"Weather, not whether you blundering buffoon! It can control the weather!"

Pat blinked but said nothing.

"It can make it rain or snow!"

"Oh!" The large man suddenly understood. He laughed as he said, "Why didn't you say so!"

Phineas sighed as he set his tea aside and picked up the mail-order catalog, flipping to the order page. "Patrick, take this with you. Send the order by wire to this company and make sure they understand we need the shipment before the twenty-fourth."

The bearded man took the catalog, tucking it under his arm. "Cutting it close, ain't we?"

"Which is why," Phineas said, holding up a finger, "you will also tell them that one of Jed's airships will be dispatched to collect the order as soon as it arrives at the depot. No excuses, no delays."

Pat grinned. "Alright, Hargy. I'll get it sent straightaway."

"Bully," Phineas replied, already turning back toward his invention. "Now, go on. I've important adjustments to make."

Pat gave the contraption one last curious glance before stepping out into the afternoon light. The barn door thumped shut behind him, leaving Phineas alone with his creation.

With deliberate care, he took a cloth and polished the brass and copper of the compact weather machine. He adjusted a pair of tiny valves, gave the top gauge a tap with his finger, and then reached for a brass lever on the back side.

The hum from within deepened, a faint whirring joining the sound as the weathervane on top spun faster. A moment later, the air above the machine shimmered—and then, to Phineas' satisfaction, delicate white flakes began drifting down.

Within seconds, the hay-strewn dirt floor of the Davenport barn started gathering a light dusting of snow. It swirled gently in the beams of sunlight slanting through the loft, catching in Panther's fur and settling on Dottie's round belly.

Phineas clasped his hands behind his back, surveying the scene with pride. "Yes," he murmured, "this year's Christmas party will be nothing short of spectacular."

He reached for one of the *fancy cookies* as he sipped his tea. Immediately, he spat it out as he realized he had just placed a small fish in his mouth. He whirled his head and looked at the tray. Next to his saucer and plate of cookies was a bowl of sardines.

"These must be yours!" He set the dish down on the floor. The two cats immediately jumped off the settee and ran toward it.

Phineas wiped off his hands and continued to enjoy his tea and biscuits.

Minutes later, the sound of a horse galloping up was heard. It was accompanied by the jingle of the harness. Right after this, the barn door creaked open. A gust of cold air swept in as Tom Miller stepped through, brushing dust from his coat. His cheeks were pink from the ride, and a scarf was wound haphazardly around his neck.

"Afternoon, Professor," he said, glancing down as a snowflake landed on the brim of his hat. He frowned, brushing it away. "Does the barn have a hole in the roof... wait... it wasn't snowing when I rode up..."

Phineas glanced over at the young man, the faintest smirk curling his mustache. "It might not be snowing out there, but as you can see, it is in here."

Tom stepped further inside, his boots crunching faintly on the dusting of white across the barn floor. He glanced toward the pot-belly stove where Panther and Dottie had taken refuge. "How?"

"Science." Phineas clasped his hands behind his back and rocked on his heels, clearly pleased with himself. "After last year's long, bitter winter, one might think I'd be grateful for a mild December. Yet, as you've no doubt noticed, there isn't so much as a single flake on the eaves."

Tom shrugged. "Can't say I mind, myself."

"That is because you lack vision, my dear boy," Phineas said grandly. "Imagine it—a perfect white Christmas, snowflakes drifting down over the entire ranch while the guests arrive, sleigh bells in the distance. A scene to warm even the most stoniest of hearts."

Tom tilted his head, watching a flake melt on his glove. "You did this?"

"With the aid of this," Phineas gestured toward the brass-and-copper box, its weathervane turning steadily.

"This meteorological marvel is what I fondly call my *Atmospheric Regulator*," he gave the side a fond pat, "patent pending, of course. This will be my gift to everyone at Davenport Ranch this year. The most perfect gift anyone could possibly give."

Tom chuckled, looking around the barn as the snow continued to fall. "Well, I gotta hand it to you, Professor. If this works outside the barn like it does in here, you might just pull it off."

"I have no doubt it will work," Phineas said proudly.

"Have you thought about sharing this with the whole valley?" Eighteen-year-old Tom Miller asked curiously. "You could give all of Spoon Fork a white Christmas."

Phineas thought about it for a moment. You could see the wheels spinning inside his head. He opened his mouth and was just about to speak when suddenly Pat came bursting back into the room, cheeks flushed from the cold and scarf trailing behind him.

"Wire's sent!" he announced, suddenly shivering as he began to get covered in a light dusting. "But you'll never guess what came in over the telegraph..."

He stopped mid-sentence, squinting at the barn's interior. "Now hold on... It wasn't snowin' when I left a few minutes ago!"

"Pat," Tom grinned. "Don't tell me you've never heard of Fabulous Phineas Hargroves' Atmospheric Conjurator."

Pat peered suspiciously at the brass-and-copper box. "Fabulous Phineas Hargroves' Atmospheric Con... con ju... con ju rate or?"

"That's not even what it's called, let alone how you pronounce it!" Phineas puffed up like a rooster in full crow. "My good man, the feat you are witnessing is my genius at work. I have merely harnessed the untamed forces of nature for the betterment of mankind—specifically for the holiday spirit. Behold!" He spread his arms through the falling flakes. "My *Atmospheric Regulator*!"

Pat just stared. "So you're tellin' me your snow-making machine actually works?"

"It doesn't just make snow, Patrick," Phineas said, his voice dropping to a reverent tone. "An instrument of precision. Rain, sleet, snow—any atmospheric condition I choose, right at my fingertips. Just think of all the benefits this will provide. For instance, no more crops ruined due to extreme temperatures and long periods of drought."

"Gosh!" Pat whistled. "And to think earlier you didn't even know whether it was going to work or not."

Trying to ignore that statement, Professor Hargroves suddenly asked about the telegraph Pat mentioned when he first barged in.

"Jumpin' Jehoshaphat!" Pat exclaimed. "I clean forgot!" He suddenly held the paper out in front of him. Phineas immediately snatched it out of his hand and began reading it. "It's from Jed! He and Matt are stuck in Windmire Junction. Some nasty business with sabotage and a boiler explosion."

"Boiler explosion." Tom whistled low. "Are they okay?"

"It says they're fine." Phineas continued reading. "They just need replacement parts and..." He cut his sentence short as he turned and saw Pat Bennington crouched beside the brass-and-copper box, peering at its gauges with a childlike fascination.

"What happens if I turn this here all the way up?" Pat asked, fingers already curling around the main lever.

"Pat!" Phineas lunged forward, but it was too late.

With a decisive click, the *Atmospheric Regulator* gave a sharp hiss, the hum within rising to a fever pitch. The weathervane atop the chimney spun so fast it blurred. A sudden gust roared through the barn, whipping hay into the air and scattering loose tools across the floor.

Snowflakes became a torrent, swirling in thick, wind-driven sheets. The temperature plunged, their breath instantly visible in the frigid air. Panther and Dottie dove under the settee, and Tom yanked his scarf tighter around his neck.

The walls of the barn began to creak as the wind increased. They were now in the middle of a fierce indoor winter storm!

With a decisive click, the
Atmospheric Regulator gave a sharp hiss,
the hum within rising to a fever pitch.
The weathervane atop the chimney
spun so fast it blurred.

CHAPTER IV

The Lone Outlaw

"Patrick, shut it off! Shut it off this instant!" Phineas barked, struggling toward the controls through the miniature blizzard.

But Pat was doing all he could to stand up against the gale winds. "It's like a hurricane but with snow!"

The stove rattled under the strain of the cold, a bucket of nails tipped over in the loft, and snow piled rapidly along the doors and walls, trapping them inside. The storm was building into a full squall now, the barn groaning as the wind rattled the walls and tore through the rafters.

Phineas bent down and battled his way against the fierce elements, his fingers almost closing on the lever when he was knocked backwards by a footstool flying through the air.

****

Meanwhile, as the barn blizzard grew in intensity, about ninety miles north west of Davenport ranch, the December sun was hanging low but still sharp in the pale sky. Its light cutting across an empty stone quarry. Shadows stretched long against the jagged cliffs, cold and gray, though the air itself carried only a brittle edge rather than true chill.

Two-Gun Kate sat tall in the saddle, her brown duster flaring with each gust, brass goggles glinting from the brim of her hat. Beneath her, the black stallion Bandit surged forward with long, powerful strides, mane whipping like smoke. No posse trailed her, no gang rode at her side. She was the Lone Outlaw, and that suited her just fine.

At the quarry's center sat the captured Davenport freight wagon. It was nestled next to an old wooden cabin and a couple more hijacked buckboards. Behind the shack was a makeshift corral housing all the stolen horses.

She swung down, her duster catching the light, walked to the nearest crate, and gave it the once over. Dashing inside, she returned moments later with a pry bar. The boards groaned under her gloved hand as she pried them open. A scatter of wooden toys and bright cloth spilled out, their cheerful hues oddly jarring against the bleak stone walls.

"Just trinkets," she muttered, carefully placing

them to the side. The next crate was filled with more toys. Another was filled with fruit cakes wrapped in cheesecloth. After opening several more, she found what she was looking for. Half a dozen wooden crates lined the bottom. They felt far heavier than they should, considering they were filled with bolts of fabric. Gently laying the material to the side, she discovered a false bottom in each of them.

One by one, Two-Gun held up futuristic-looking weapons far more advanced than the revolvers she carried on her sides. The afternoon light glistened off each one. She grinned, sharp and sure. "Now this is what I was looking for."

Kate carefully aimed a handheld atomic blaster at a nearby boulder. After adjusting the intensity down to zero, she fired. Nothing spectacular happened. She raised the weapon and fired again, but this time held her finger on the trigger longer. The red laser beam continued to focus on the boulder. After about thirty or forty seconds, it began to glow red with heat.

"That could come in handy on a cold night..." The outlaw mused, then turned the intensity all the way up to ten. Once again, she aimed and fired. This time, the boulder exploded into a thousand pieces. Small fragments rained down everywhere.

Her faithful steed began rearing and whinnying. Two-Gun immediately raced to his side to calm

The boulder exploded into a thousand pieces.
Small fragments rained down everywhere.

him.

"Easy, boy!" She said softly and gently as she patted his side. "Guess I'd better turn that dial back down." She replaced the six-gun in her holster with the blaster. It was a perfect fit. She walked back to the wagon and pulled out another one that she swapped her other pistol for.

After stashing her revolvers in a safe place, she dragged the crates off the wagon one by one and carried them safely into her little cabin. She stacked them up alongside several others.

The wood door creaked on its hinges as she shouldered it open. Inside, the air was stale with the smell of old timber, kerosene, and dust that clung to every surface. The low support beams made it possible for her to reach up and touch the ceiling.

At five foot two, she wasn't used to feeling this tall, but the cramped space had a way of pressing in. A rusted lantern hung crooked from a nail, its glass cloudy with soot, and a cast iron stove sat in the corner, its iron belly waiting to be fed. Crates and scraps of stone littered the floor, relics of the quarrymen who had once called this outpost their shelter.

For a brief moment, she wondered what had become of them before shaking the thought aside. This place was hers now, and its shadows would keep her secrets.

Later, crouched by a small campfire, Two-Gun

picked up her coffee pot and poured herself a cup. The heat from the fire barely touched the surrounding air—winter had the land in its grip, even without snow.

"They said I'd never make it as an outlaw," she said softly to the flames. "But I think this proves them all wrong."

In the distance, two faint shapes moved across the ridge. Once again, her horse began to whinny as the silhouette of two riders came into view.

"Easy, Bandit." Two-Gun Kate smiled. "I was expecting these two."

Despite being relatively confident they were who she thought they were, Kate's hand continued to linger on the blaster at her hip as Bandit pawed nervously at the ground.

Moments later, as the riders descended, their details came clear. Thomas Avery and Mr. Pierce, still dressed in their neatly pressed suits and derby hats, their overcoats once again buttoned tight against the brittle air. They looked painfully overdressed for the quarry, like bankers who had wandered into the woods by mistake.

Kate smirked, brushing a fleck of dust from her coat. "It's about time," she murmured.

The riders drew rein a few yards away. Avery removed his hat with stiff formality, though his eyes flicked uneasily toward the shattered boulder. Pierce, ever more taciturn, kept a gloved hand near his coat pocket as though the cold weren't the only thing making him fidget.

"You're late," Kate said flatly, folding her arms across her chest.

"We had to take care of a few things in town before we came out," Pierce explained.

"I was starting to wonder if Mayor Windmire had caught on to us." Two-Gun eyed them both suspiciously.

"On the contrary," Thomas Avery replied, his voice calm but thin in the open air. "The mayor hasn't a clue that either one of us is connected to you. We've got him convinced we're on his side." Thomas glanced again at the empty wagon. "Were they carrying what we suspected?"

Kate's grin widened. "You tell me..." She drew one of the blasters and aimed at a nearby tree, adjusted the intensity, and sliced it in half with one pass. It fell in a clearing away from them.

Avery whistled as he pushed his hat back. "*The Clockwork Conqueror* certainly knew his stuff!"

Kate's eyes glanced at Pierce, who was still holding his hand near his coat pocket.

"I can assure you," she smiled. "You won't need that derringer!"

Moving his hand away, he nervously replied. "Can't be too cautious in our line of work. Can't trust anyone!"

Two-Gun laughed as she holstered her blaster.

"Understandable."

"What about the lockbox filled with donations for the orphanage?" Thomas asked, as if he suddenly remembered it and it wasn't consistently on his mind the entire ride over.

Kate turned and picked up a metal box she had resting on the ground next to her. The lock had been shot off.

"It was wrapped in a bolt of yard goods." She explained as she tossed it to him.

Avery took one look inside and then asked, "Is this some kind of joke?" He held up a stack of newspaper cut to the size of paper money.

****

Meanwhile, just a few miles away, the gas lamps of Windmire Junction flickered to life, their glow casting amber pools along the frozen boardwalks. In a corner hotel room overlooking the main street, Jedidiah Davenport sat slouched in a chair, a damp towel pressed to his temple. Across the room, Matthew Colton sat on his bed reading the local newspaper. The air still carried the tang of smoke and scorched iron from the Swift's explosion earlier that day.

Matt peered over the top of the paper, frowning. "Well, we made the front page."

"Our meeting with the Mayor?"

"No, the explosion." Matt flipped through the paper. "The meeting with the Mayor got pushed down a few pages."

"I'm sure Windmire will be thrilled about that." Jedidiah shrugged. "Any mention of how they plan to track down the saboteurs?"

"They don't..." Matthew Colton took a deep breath before explaining. "They have it made out like it was negligence on our fault. They've made us out to be fools who can't keep a boiler in one piece."

"Yes, because risking our necks and blowing up the ship sounds like such a fine idea," Jed muttered. He set the towel aside and leaned forward, elbows on his knees. "If it weren't for the promises we made to the orphanage, as soon as the Swift was repaired, I'd get out of this town and never come back."

"I'm for that!"

"I wonder if the telegraph office has received Phineas' reply yet."

"You know the professor. He's liable to not respond at all and just come flying in at the last moment." Matt grinned mischievously. "Assuming he doesn't get distracted by another one of his inventions."

"You're right." Jed exhaled sharply, half a laugh, half a sigh. "Knowing him, he's probably not even read it and is blissfully tinkering away as we speak."

Matt flipped to another section, his brow tightening. "And here's something else… they've got another column about that outlaw."

Jedidiah glanced up. "Two-Gun Kate?"

"Yeah. They've given her a second name. They're calling her the *Lone Outlaw* out of irony. Says there's no way she's pulling off all of these heists on her own. She's been holding up every shipment in or out of Windmire Junction for a few weeks now." He shook his head. "Seems like every paper wants to turn her into a legend."

Jed muttered as he reached for his cup of tea. "Legends are the last thing we need right now."

After taking a sip, he stood up and moved to the bureau under the window and slid a folded packet of blueprints into one of the drawers.

"What's that?" Matt asked, lowering the paper.

"Phineas' steam-powered tractor design. I promised to send it by mail to the patent office for him."

After this, he reached up, parted the curtain with two fingers, and looked out. That's when he spotted a strange man staring back at him from another building across the street. "Looks like we've got ourselves a Peeping Tom." He glanced back at Matthew.

"You sure?"

"Come here and take a look for yourself..." The

young entrepreneur glanced back, but the person in the window was gone. "That's odd..."

Suddenly, a knock rattled the hotel door. Both men stiffened. Jed looked around for one of the paralyzing ray guns he normally carried with him. He'd forgotten he'd left them stowed away aboard the Swift. Meanwhile, Matt folded his newspaper and set it aside, moving as silently as a cat toward the wall.

"Mr. Davenport, Mr. Colton," came a muffled voice. "It's Mr. Wainwright from the front desk. A messenger just dropped off an invitation for you."

Jed glanced at Matt, who shook his head slowly. "An invitation?" he called. "From who?" he asked the clerk.

A pause. "Looks like it's from the Mayor."

"Windmire?" Jed asked.

The clerk's eyes lit up. "The one and only! Mayor Silas T. Windmire himself. Finest man this town's ever had in office, if you ask me!"

Most folks in town spoke of Mayor Windmire with the same kind of admiration. His charm and confidence had won them over completely. They hung on his every word and trusted his judgment without question. Anyone who dared speak against him or his policies usually found themselves on the outside looking in.

Jedidiah groaned as he opened the door and reached for the paper. "Thank you," He remarked as he tried to re-close it, but Wainwright cleared his throat and held his hand out.

"He wants a tip, Jed." Matthew smiled.

"Oh! Yes, of course!" Davenport fumbled around his pockets, but the smallest thing he could find was a silver dollar. "I'm afraid I don't have anything smaller than..."

"Thank you, Sir!" Wainwright cut him off and snatched the coin from his hand. "Your generosity won't be forgotten!" He immediately turned on his heel and retreated down the hall.

"I was going to ask for change..." Jed groaned as he closed the door and turned back to his childhood friend.

"Maybe next time lead with that?" Matt chuckled as he glanced at the envelope. "Where have we been invited?"

"Town Hall for dinner," Jedidiah replied as he sat down, leaned forward in the chair, and reached for the pair of shoes sitting neatly at his feet. The leather gleamed in the lamplight, the burgundy, mustard yellow, and sky-blue panels catching his eye the way they always did—bold and unapologetic, just like their owner.

He slid his foot in, gave his heel a firm tap on the floor, and tied the lace. The second followed just as quickly. When he stood, the bold mix of red, yellow, and blue flashed beneath his trousers, loud as a declaration.

Matt's brow furrowed as he came over. "I thought we were just going to have a steak down in the hotel dining room." He seemed disappointed.

"Maybe the Mayor will be serving steak." Jed turned on his heel and started towards the door. "Either way, who am I to pass up a free meal?"

"Well, now that you put it that way..." Matthew Colton chuckled. "As long as we don't have to dress up like we did for that Masquerade Ball back in Detroit!"

"It doesn't mention anything about dressing for dinner on the invitation," Jedidiah replied, as he folded the paper and stuck it in his pocket. "Besides, these fancy shoes are the most I'm dressing up tonight!"

Both men laughed heartily, and Jed reached for the door. Before he could open it, faint voices drifted up from the street below.

At first, it was just a low harmony—but then it grew clearer, rich with the sound of many voices blending together.

Matthew rushed to the window and looked out. A group of carolers had gathered beneath the hotel's front awning, their breath puffing white in the cold air as they sang.

"*God Rest Ye Merry, Gentlemen, let nothing you dismay…*"

The familiar refrain floated through the frosted windowpanes, accompanied by the faint jingle of a handbell keeping time.

Jed paused, one hand resting on the knob. "Well, that's something we don't get to hear out at the ranch," he said softly.

"Maybe that's a good thing." Matt smiled faintly, glancing toward the sound. "Imagine Pat, or your foreman Jim Davis, and the other ranch hands all trying to harmonize."

"I'd rather not." Jed laughed. "Come on, let's not keep the Mayor waiting."

With that, he grabbed his cap with the goggles firmly attached and pushed open the door. The chorus of carolers began lilting up the stairs. It sounded like they had entered the lobby.

He stepped into the dimly lit hall, then turned back to make sure Matt was behind him. That's when someone in the shadows stepped forward and hit him over the back of the head. As he started to fall, they grabbed him under his arms and dragged him away.

Not realizing what just happened, Matthew Colton happily stepped into the hallway. He turned to look for Jed. That's when a second person stepped from the shadows and clubbed him.

CHAPTER V

Bound and Determined

Sometime later, the two daring young men began to stir. Jedidiah Davenport was first, his head pounding like a boiler about to burst. The air around him was thick and stale, laced with the scent of damp earth and old stone. He tried to move, only to feel the bite of rope digging into his wrists and ankles, securely bound.

A groan came from his right. "Jed? That you?" It was Matthew Colton, his voice muffled and groggy.

"Yeah. Don't move too quickly." Jedidiah tested the ropes, the fibers creaking as he twisted against them. His back was pressed to a cold stone wall. "Can you see anything?"

"Not much. Just shadows." Matt shifted, and the scrape of boot leather against dirt echoed across the room. "I think we're in a cellar."

Jed tried to make out details in the darkness. A

faint glimmer of lamplight leaked under a door across the room. The smell of kerosene lingered, mingling with dust and mildew. Wooden crates were stacked haphazardly along one wall, their stenciled labels unreadable in the gloom.

"Wherever we are," Jed muttered, "we didn't come here of our own free will." Suddenly, he turned his head toward a wall with a small window near the ceiling. It was very dirty and allowed very little light to pass through. Still, Davenport noticed he could hear familiar sounds coming from it.

"Do you hear that?" he asked.

"The carolers!" Matthew replied excitedly.

"That means we may still be in the hotel," Jed tried to rise, but the rope around his ankles sent him toppling back hard against the stone wall. Dust shook loose from the ceiling.

"*Sizzling steam pipes!*" he exclaimed. "Matt, come help me."

"Okay," Matthew scooted closer, the scrape of rope against rope rasping in the gloom. "But, I'm just as bound as you are. I don't know how you think I can help."

"I've got an idea." Jed craned his neck toward him. "Let's get back to back. We can push each other up."

Awkwardly, they shuffled around until their shoulders touched. Muscles straining, they bent their knees, pressed together, and heaved upward.

Their boots slipped on the damp earth, ropes cutting deeper into their wrists. For a moment, it seemed to work—their backs straightened, spines locking together like a brace. Then Matt's foot slid in the dirt, and the two of them pitched sideways in a heap.

"Well, that didn't work," Matthew grunted, spitting dust.

"I have another idea," Jed muttered, rolling onto his side. "Come closer. If you twist around, maybe I can work at the knots around your wrists with my fingers."

It took some doing, but Matthew wriggled around until his bound hands were brushing against Jed's fingertips. Davenport twisted, clawed, and tugged, sweat beading on his brow.

"Anything?" Jed asked, straining to keep his voice down.

"Almost there," Matt replied. "I feel the rope loosening." He gave a sudden yank, and one of the knots slipped just enough for his wrists to slide out.

"Got it!" Colton immediately reached down and undid the rope around his own ankles before turning to work on Davenport's ropes.

A few moments later, Jed's wrists came free. He shook the blood back into his hands, flexing his sore fingers. Then he undid his own ankles.

Both men sat there, rubbing raw wrists, the faint sound of voices still drifting through the cellar window.

"Well," Jed whispered, finally allowing himself a thin smile, "let's find our way out of here."

The carolers' song rose faintly, muffled through the grime-streaked window. Jed and Matthew exchanged a knowing glance. The hotel carried on with its festive hum, none the wiser that two men had been dragged below.

****

While Jedidiah and Matthew were still orienting themselves with their surroundings, the barn blizzard incident back at the ranch had already been resolved.

It was there, hours after the event occurred, that the rattle of wagon wheels announced Professor Phineas B. Hargroves' return. He came riding up to the stately Victorian manor in a black-topped buggy that creaked along the frozen ground. The tired horse stamped against the chill, steam curling from its nostrils. Phineas, reins loose in hand, looked every bit the weary traveler. His boots, however, betrayed him—mud-streaked, dust-caked, and scuffed, as though he had left the buggy long behind and struck out across hill and stone on foot.

Pat Bennington came out on the porch with a tray of sandwiches for Tom Miller, whom Phineas had put in charge of loading the boiler onto the

Icarus.

"Mind giving me a ride to your hangar?" the rotund man asked. "That young feller up there must be starving by now!"

Phineas merely nodded his head and motioned to the space beside him. "I was just about to head there myself." he remarked.

When they reached the large structure, the faint glow of lanterns revealed Tom and the automatons hard at work inside. The gleaming frames of the mechanical men moved deliberately, loading crates and brass fittings into the belly of the Icarus. Tom Miller, sleeves rolled to the elbow, wiped a smear of grease from his jaw as he barked an order to one of the machines.

"Hey Tom!" Pat called out. "How's about takin' a break and eatin' some grub!"

"Glad to!" the dark-haired eighteen-year-old smiled as he poured some water from a pitcher into a bowl and began to wash up.

Phineas reached over for one of the multitude of sandwiches on the tray, but Pat immediately slapped his hand.

"Those are for Tom!" he scolded, snatching the sandwich the professor had been reaching for and stuck it in his own mouth.

"But there are so many of them..." Hargroves cut his sentence short as he watched Pat devour the entire thing in two bites. "Egads!"

"What?" The rotund man laughed. "I worked up quite an appetite throwing these things together!"

"Can't I at least have one?"

"Tell you what, Hargy." Pat waved the tray temptingly close. "If you tell me how you managed to get that snow-making machine of yours turned off earlier, I'll let you have one."

Phineas groaned and shook his head. His voice was cool and precise. "I would prefer it if you never spoke of that incident again."

Pat stumbled over his words. "But... but... I just wanted to know, how in blazes did you shut that infernal contraption down?"

"My dear man, you wouldn't believe me if I told you."

Pat smirked slightly. "Was it that incredible?"

Before Phineas could reply, Tom burst out laughing. He leaned against a crate, still shaking his head in disbelief.

"I saw it and I still don't believe it." The young man's laugh deepened.

"Well, now, I gotta know!"

Suddenly, Phineas stepped past both Tom Miller and Pat Bennington, his long coat brushing against the dirt floor. He cast a glance toward the Icarus. His expression betrayed neither fatigue nor satisfaction—only calculation. He could hear Cogsworth, Apollo, and Artemis all three stowing away the last of the parts below.

"Excellent work, Mr. Miller," he said briskly. "Now I suggest you board your horse in the stable if you wish to accompany me when I set sail for Windmire Junction."

The professor turned toward Pat Bennington, who was starting his third sandwich while Tom was still on his first. "Pat, be a good man and drive young Miller here back to the house. After he takes care of his horse, help him load those crates of chocolate Jed requested for the orphanage. I'll stay here and prepare my airship for departure."

Phineas waited until Pat and Tom had clambered up into the buggy, then with one swift motion, he leaned across the seat and snatched one of the sandwiches. The professor took a deliberate bite, chewing with smug satisfaction as the wheels began to creak back toward the house.

A minute later, the carriage rolled up to the rear of the stately Victorian manor, its gas lamps glowing warmly. Tom swung down the moment they arrived and hurried toward the barn, where his faithful steed still stood reined to the hitching post. The horse snorted impatiently, stamping the frozen earth, until Tom unbuckled the reins and led him inside the stables.

Pat, meanwhile, ambled up the back steps of the house, humming to himself between mouthfuls. Inside the kitchen pantry, wooden crates lined the wall, each one marked in neat stenciling: "Imported

Confectionery." With a grunt, Pat carried them one by one into the kitchen and stacked them in an uneven pile next to the wood-burning stove.

Agatha Porter entered a moment later, adjusting the bun on top of her head as she walked over.

"Pat, is that the chocolate Jed had shipped here from England?" she asked.

"Sure is!" the rotund man exclaimed. "He wants to give what's left to the youngins over at the orphanage."

"The way you and Matt have been helping yourselves, I'm surprised there's still four crates left."

"Well, one crate may or may not be mostly empty wrapping papers..." Pat admitted sheepishly.

"Why am I not surprised?" The older woman rolled her eyes. Then she suddenly realized something about the way Pat was stacking the wooden boxes.

"Do you really think it's a good idea to pile them up like that?" She looked at him, confused.

The rotund, bearded man dusted his hands on his waistcoat, beaming proudly at the leaning tower of chocolate. "Aggy, I was born with a natural gift for balance. Why, I could stack three grand pianos on top of each other and not a single key would fall out of tune!"

"It would still be the prettiest music you ever made." Agatha folded her arms, unimpressed. "But that's not what I was talking about."

Pat tucked his fingers behind his suspenders and grinned. "Aggy, quit your worrying. It'll be just fine. Now, if you'll excuse me, I'm gonna go fetch Tom and get him to help me carry everything outside."

"Pat, wait!" She called out in vain to stop him.

The bearded man ignored her as he strolled out the door, humming as always. A few minutes later, he found Tom Miller patting down his horse. Tom had just finished stabling and feeding it.

While they were there, the two of them went ahead and took care of the other horses, including Jedidiah's faithful steed, Blaze. Nearly an hour later, they started back to the house.

"Alright," Pat announced grandly as he pushed open the kitchen door, "time to haul..."

His sentence ended in a yelp as his boots shot out from under him. He landed flat on his back in a thick pool of brown liquid.

"Pat!" Tom froze in the doorway, trying to contain his laughter. "Where did that puddle of chocolate come from?"

For a moment, there was only a groan from the floor.

Bennington raised one dripping hand. It was brown, sticky, and fragrant. "Not a puddle," he groaned again. "A lake."

The rotund man glanced over at his coworker

and asked, "Aggy, what were you trying to tell me about the crates of chocolate?"

Agatha Porter stood with both arms folded, her expression exactly what Pat didn't want to see. She nodded toward the stove, where the heat shimmered against the leaning stack of crates, chocolate still oozing steadily across the kitchen floor.

"I think you've figured it out for yourself," she said crisply.

Tom laughed so hard he nearly doubled over. Agatha pinched the bridge of her nose.

Pat floundered, tried to sit up, and promptly slid again. "Well, don't just stand there, grab some cups out of the cabinet! Jed can serve everybody hot chocolate instead!"

****

In the meantime, as chocolate continued to flow like water on Davenport Ranch, miles away in Windmire Junction, the laughter and warmth of Christmas carols still drifted faintly through the hotel above. However, in the cold stone cellar, the mood was anything but festive.

Jedidiah Davenport pressed his palms against the only door in the room. Light was seeping in from under the bottom edge. He assumed this led to a staircase going back up into the hotel.

"It's locked," he whispered.

Matthew Colton, who had just used his handkerchief to clean off the window, allowing a little more light into the room, crouched by the door. He tilted his head to listen—boots scuffed against hardwood floors above them, voices murmured. They both shouted for help, but nobody seemed to hear them.

Matt nodded, rubbing his wrists. "Let's see if this door is as old as it looks." He stepped back a few paces, leaned his shoulder down, and rushed toward it. The hinges groaned, but didn't give.

"No use," the dark-haired young man groaned as he plopped down on the floor.

"Wait, Matt, give it another try!" Davenport shouted enthusiastically. "I think I heard something crack!"

"That was my shoulder..." Matt groaned. "When you get a moment, can you help me pop it back into place?"

"Oh yes, of course!" Jedidiah rushed to his friend's side and grabbed his arm, but Matthew brushed him away, saying he was exaggerating.

"But only by a little..." He quickly added.

Jed rolled his eyes as he began to pace back and forth. He rummaged through the cellar like a man possessed, brushing dust from every crate and shelf. His hand landed on a rusted lantern missing its glass, but still half full of coal oil. He gave Matt a quick grin.

"I think I just found our way out."

Matt groaned. "Jed, I don't like that look on your face. That's the same one you had right before you put that tack on the teacher's chair, and we both had to clap erasers for a week because she assumed I helped you."

Ignoring his comments, Jed grabbed his friend's handkerchief, dipped it into the lantern, and twisted it into a makeshift fuse. Next, he placed it at the base of the door just before striking a match.

"Jed!" Matt hissed, ducking behind a very large crate.

The cloth flared, the oil sizzling as the material lit up. Davenport rushed over and dove next to his childhood companion. For a long breathless moment, nothing happened. Several more went by, and still nothing.

"It didn't work..." Jed finally stood up and looked at the door.

"Can't say that I'm disappointed!" Matthew breathed a sigh of relief as he stood to his feet.

The young entrepreneur's eyes immediately started scanning the cellar again, searching for something else they could use. His gaze landed on a wooden rack in the far corner, where a dozen bottles were stacked. He rushed over, picked one up, and blew off some dust from the glass. The liquid inside sloshed dark and rich.

"Wine," he muttered.

Matthew raised a brow. "I don't think now's the best time to celebrate, Jed."

"Not for drinking," Davenport replied. He tapped the glass, listening to the hollow ring. "Wine burns like oil. Maybe we can try our explosive again with one of these."

Matt blinked. "You mean to tell me you're gonna blow the door open with a bottle of Merlot?"

Jed grinned as he wiped dust off the paper label with his sleeve. The words came into view in elegant French script: *Château Margaux, Médoc 1874.*

He gave the cork a twist and sniffed, his brow lifting. "Cabernet, if my nose is right."

Suddenly, an explosion shook the cellar. The lantern's burning cloth had been smoldering all this time—and now it finally erupted.

BOOOOOM!

The door flew open. Smoke curled upward through the splintered frame.

The shockwave hurled both young men off their feet, slamming them against one of the cellar walls.

The shockwave hurled both young men
off their feet, slamming them against
one of the cellar walls.

CHAPTER VI

Dust and Disgrace

The gas lamps lining the streets of Windmire Junction burned bright against the December night as Thomas Avery and Mr. Pierce climbed the granite steps of the Town Hall. Their polished boots rang against the marble floor of the banquet hall as they were ushered into the mayor's office.

Silas T. Windmire was pacing like a caged lion. His mustache twitched with every turn, his fists clenched behind his back.

"Where are they?" the mayor thundered. "The dinner I planned was supposed to start an hour ago, and Davenport hasn't so much as shown his face! I have two reporters waiting in the dining room to cover this meeting."

Avery bowed his head slightly, calm as ever. "Mr. Mayor, we left instructions for them to meet you here. Surely they've only been delayed."

"Delayed?" Windmire snapped, eyes flashing.

"Find them. Now! If some small-town rancher thinks he can embarrass me in my own city, he's got another thing coming."

A deep chime from the grandfather clock in the corner announced the time.

"It's already half past eight," Mayor Windmire muttered. "Bring them here immediately!"

Pierce adjusted his cuffs, his expression tight. "We'll see to it personally, sir."

Moments later, the two men were striding down the gaslit street toward the hotel. The lobby clerk stiffened at their approach, fumbling with his registry book until Avery's sharp gaze froze him in place.

"Key," Avery said flatly. "Davenport and Colton's room. Now!"

The man swallowed, handed it over, and pointed toward the staircase. "Third floor, west wing…"

They didn't bother thanking him.

When they reached the room, the door was ajar. Inside, drawers had been pulled out, clothes scattered across the floor. A chair lay on its side, covered in bed sheets.

Pierce's eyes narrowed. "This is a disaster!"

From the far corner came a shuffling sound. Two rough-looking men—jackets rumpled, hats askew—froze mid-search when the door slammed back against the wall. One of them had a set of

Jedidiah's papers half-stuffed into his pocket.

"Well," Avery said coolly, stepping inside, "what do the two of you have to say for yourselves?"

The taller thug stammered, "We were just—just following orders."

"Whose orders?" Pierce snapped.

"Yours!" the smaller one blurted out. "You told us to go through their things..."

"While they were at dinner with the mayor! You were supposed to follow them and make sure they made it." Avery's jaw tightened, though his voice stayed calm. "And yet somehow they never showed up!"

The thugs exchanged uneasy glances. The taller one cleared his throat. "We might've... uh... misunderstood our instructions."

Pierce's tone was ice. "Misunderstood?"

"We sorta subdued them, you might say..."

"Subdued?"

"Tied 'em up and dragged 'em down to the cellar. Figured as long as they were unconscious anyway, we might as well."

"Unconscious?" Mr. Pierce reluctantly asked.

"We sorta knocked them out..."

"You imbeciles!" Avery hissed. "You were told to follow and then search the room, not assault them!"

The smaller thug shuffled his feet. "We didn't

mean any harm. Just thought this way was faster."

Avery drew a slow breath, smoothing his gloves as though steadying himself. "If Davenport suspects we were behind this, it will ruin everything. Do you grasp the danger you've put us in?"

Neither man answered.

Pierce leaned closer, his voice low and dangerous. "Pray they don't escape before we can find them, or it won't be Windmire you'll have to fear."

The thugs paled.

"Did you at least find anything important?"

"Just these papers..."

Thomas Avery grabbed the documents from his hand, straightened himself, and forced his composure back into place. "Very well. They're in the cellar, you say?"

Both nodded quickly.

"You obviously had some way to sneak them down there without arousing suspicion," Mr. Pierce spoke up. "We hired you because you both used to work in this hotel. You obviously know your way around. How do we get down to the cellar from this floor?"

"There's a staircase in the back of the linen closet at the end of the hall on every floor. It's for staff only."

"I want the two of you to clean this mess up,"

Avery ordered.

"After that, I want you both out of town before anyone can link us together!" Pierce said, thrusting an envelope at them. Inside was the pay they'd been promised.

Avery turned toward his cohort. "Come, Mr. Pierce. We'll fetch them before the mayor suspects we're involved."

"How will we explain this to them?"

"We'll figure it out on the way!"

The two men rushed down the hall, leaving the hired thugs behind.

****

Meanwhile, several floors below them, smoke curled upward from the shattered doorway. Jedidiah Davenport coughed hard, rolling onto his side as he tried to blink the grit out of his eyes. The explosion still rang in his ears.

"Matt..." he rasped, clutching his ribs. "You alive?"

A groan answered him. Matthew Colton staggered to his knees, brushing ash from his hair. "Barely. How much of that wine did we have?"

"None," Jed Davenport tried to laugh, but it came out as another cough. Pulling himself upright, he saw the cellar door hanging crooked on one hinge, light spilling in from the hallway beyond.

"Looks like we found our way out," Jed said, still grinning despite the pain.

"Good," Matthew muttered, rubbing his shoulder. "Now maybe you can carry me out of here."

"Carry you?" Jedidiah looked concerned. "Are you hurt?"

"No," the dark-haired young man smiled. "Just thought it was worth a try."

Suddenly, heavy boots creaked across the floorboards above. Both looked toward the ceiling.

"Do you think whoever locked us in here heard the explosion?" Matthew asked, his voice low and uneasy.

"I don't know, but I don't feel like sticking around and explaining things to the hotel staff." Jed chuckled as he rushed towards the ruined doorway. Matthew Colton followed close behind.

They pushed through the splintered frame into cooler air. The cellar gave way to a narrow corridor stretching ahead, shadows clinging to the corners. Several sets of staircases led to different levels of the hotel.

"Which one should we take?" Jedidiah asked his childhood friend.

"I vote for the one closest to us!" Matthew replied as he started up the flight of steps to his immediate right.

As they moved along, every creak of the stairs

made them flinch, half-expecting armed men to appear at any second. At the top, faint light flickered under a door, and the muffled sound of voices carried through the wood.

Jedidiah held up a hand, his expression stern. "This is it. You ready?"

Matthew gave a quick nod, flexing his sore shoulder. "On three."

They braced themselves, each taking a side of the frame. Jed counted softly, "One... two... three!"

With a shove, they burst through the door and charged into—

—the hotel kitchen.

Steam hissed from a row of kettles. Pots clattered on the stove. A cook in a flour-streaked apron spun around, ladle in hand, eyes wide. Beside him, a young waiter nearly dropped a tray stacked with plates.

For a heartbeat, everyone froze, staring at each other.

Jed cleared his throat. "Uh... afternoon, gentlemen."

The cook blinked. "What are you doing charging into my galley like a pair of lunatics?"

Matthew and Jed exchanged a knowing glance. "Guess this isn't quite the outlaw hideout we were afraid of bursting into."

"Outlaw hideout!" The cook fumed. "This

happens to be a respectful hotel! Now, kindly get out of my kitchen before I have you thrown out!" He waved his soup ladle in the air like a weapon. A nearby waiter muttered something about fetching the manager.

"Time to go," Jedidiah whispered, grabbing Matthew's sleeve.

They ducked past the swinging doors before anyone could stop them. A startled maid yelped as they nearly bowled her over in the hallway, but the two men didn't slow down until they burst into the lobby.

The glittering chandeliers and polished marble floor were a stark contrast to the smoke-stained cellar they'd just escaped. But they had no time to take in the change of scenery, because standing at the center of the lobby were Thomas Avery and Mr. Pierce.

Both men were sharp as ever, derby hats perched neatly on their heads, their expressions cool and unreadable. They looked frantic until they spotted Jed and Matt.

"Mr. Davenport. Mr. Colton." Avery's voice carried, calm and clipped. "You're late. Mayor Windmire has been expecting you."

Jedidiah glanced at Matthew, who was still brushing soot off his coat. "Dinner," he muttered under his breath. "I completely forgot."

Pierce's eyes flicked toward the grime, the ash,

the disheveled state of their outfits. "Your clothes are disgraceful, but we don't have time for you to change..."

Jed straightened his cap, forcing a polite smile. "I appreciate you making allowances for us..."

"Sod busters?" Thomas Avery finished his sentence.

"I was going to say we had run into a little trouble, but..."

"What do you mean by sod buster?" Matthew leaped between Jedidiah and the two men. He was fuming mad.

"Well, after all, you both do look like you've just come straight from the fields of your farm."

"It's a ranch, not a farm." Jedidiah smiled, trying to remain calm. "Also, the reason why we look the way we do is because..."

"Oh, pish posh!" This time, Avery spoke up, interrupting Jed. "We don't have time for your quaint musings. Mayor Windmire is waiting, so please save us the details of your grim little story."

"Well, do we at least have time to go to our room and wash up before we go?" Colton moved forward, ready to fight.

Both polished men exchanged a nervous glance, and Mr. Pierce fumbled over his words. "Really, gentlemen. Do you really expect to keep Mayor Silas T. Windmire waiting while you freshen up?"

Matthew took another step towards the two

men, and Jedidiah immediately moved in front of him. "I'm sure we can wash up at the Mayor's house." He placed a hand on his friend's shoulder, trying to calm him. Matthew took a deep breath, then reluctantly agreed.

****

Minutes later, Thomas Avery and Mr. Pierce ushered Jedidiah and Matthew through the grand entryway of the recently renovated Town Hall. Crystal sconces blazed along the paneled walls, their light splintering across gold-trimmed mirrors that multiplied the glow a dozen times over. Velvet curtains pooled heavily against the floor, their tassels thick enough to serve as ropes. A chandelier hung overhead, its arms dripping with crystal drops that rattled faintly when the front door shut. Paintings crowded the walls—landscapes, hunting scenes, and, most prominently, a grand oil portrait of Silas T. Windmire himself, gazing down at visitors with studied authority.

Jedidiah and Matthew looked wildly out of place as they stepped inside—soot streaked across their cheeks, coats smudged with ash, boots leaving faint dust prints on the polished marble floor.

Silas T. Windmire emerged from the parlor as they entered, his expression easing for the briefest moment.

Windmire Junction's Town Hall.

"Ah, Davenport! You made it!" Relief briefly flickered across his face, then he froze solid when he caught sight of their appearance. His mustache twitched. "Good heavens. The two of you look like chimney sweeps."

Windmire briefly lost focus and began to mutter half to himself, half to his guests. "Did you know they only just outlawed children working as chimney sweeps in England about six years ago? Around 1875, I believe. Could you imagine the children of this fair city clambering through flues, covered head to toe in soot? I've had a few voters suggest to me that the orphans might need to be put to work if we can't replace the donations."

The mayor waved a hand dismissively, catching himself before the words could land too heavily.

"A cruel notion, of course," he laughed, "but look at you two! I'd swear you'd been crawling around in the coal mines."

Jed opened his mouth to explain, but Windmire cut him off. "Speaking of coal mines, I've had offers from the mining company to employ some of the smaller boys to work in the shafts too narrow for grown men."

"Well, thankfully, that day will never come!" Davenport stated firmly as he placed a hand on Matthew's shoulder to keep him calm.

Windmire didn't respond. He had already turned his attention toward Avery and Pierce. "Why didn't either of you mention earlier that my guests had taken up manual labor?"

Pierce said nothing. Avery merely dropped his head in silence.

The mayor turned back and gave them a curt once-over. "At the very least, wash your hands and face before the reporters see you. I won't have this press opportunity turned into a fiasco." He gestured toward a side hall where a basin of water sat next to fresh towels.

Before either man could make a move toward it, the sound of footsteps pounding across the floor caught their attention. Suddenly, two reporters burst through the open doorway, pushing aside the heavy curtain. One had a notebook in his hand, the other was carrying a large wooden camera on a matching tripod.

"Mr. Mayor," one said briskly, "we can't wait any longer. We're about to miss our deadline. The paper will be going to press soon. We'll need the photograph now."

Windmire blinked, caught off guard. "But my guests!"

The other reporter was already setting up, pulling the flash pan into place. His gaze swept across Jedidiah and Matthew, lingering with undisguised satisfaction. "Well, they certainly embody the rugged frontier look."

Jed stiffened, brushing ineffectively at the soot

on his sleeve. "Now wait just a..."

The camera was aimed at them. The mayor saw it coming, and with a practiced politician's reflexes, he swept forward, planting himself squarely between Jedidiah and Matthew, one hand around each of their shoulders. The flash went off, bathing the room in a blinding white glare. Smoke from the flash powder made them start coughing.

When Jed's vision cleared, the reporters were already packing up. "Much obliged, Mr. Mayor," one said, doffing his hat. "We'll run it on the front page tomorrow morning."

Windmire's mustache bristled. "What about the interview?"

"No time, sir. We'll schedule a meeting with you at the courthouse later this week." And with that, both men were gone, the door swinging shut behind them.

For a long moment, deafening silence hung in the glittering parlor as no one knew what to say. Finally, Windmire turned sharply to Avery and Pierce, his smile completely gone. "Gentlemen. See Mr. Davenport and Mr. Colton out!"

As they were being pushed into the street, Jedidiah drew a breath to protest, but Matthew beat him to it, his tone dry. "Does this mean we don't get dinner?"

The only answer they received was the slam of the heavy door closing in their faces.

CHAPTER VII

The Haunting Voice

Early the next morning, December 20th, 1881, light slanted through the tall windows of the Windmire Hotel, cutting across the dusty clothes Jedidiah Davenport and Matthew Colton had tossed over a couple of chairs the night before. Jedidiah stirred, groaning as he slowly blinked awake, the faint clip-clop of horses pulling wagons on the street below carrying through the glass.

The other bed in the room was empty.

Davenport pushed up on one elbow, his hair mussed, and spotted Colton already standing at the washbasin. He was dressed sharply, in a clean shirt, a brushed coat, and boots polished to a shine, calmly tightening the knot of his necktie.

"You're up early," Jedidiah muttered, scrubbing a hand across his face.

Matthew gave him a pointed look in the mirror. "Some of us don't like making our grand entrance to the breakfast table looking like a couple of chimney sweeps."

Jed winced, remembering the mayor's remarks the night before. "I paid for us each to have a hot bath last night, didn't I? Except for our dirty clothes, we left most of that coal dust behind." He swung his legs over the side of the bed. His stomach was rumbling from hunger. After they had freshened up the night before, it was too late to get any dinner. "What time is it?"

"Nearly six o'clock," Matthew replied, smoothing his hair. "Breakfast's calling my name. You'd better hurry if you want to eat with me."

Jedidiah grumbled but dragged himself to his feet, reaching for a fresh shirt. As he dressed, he glanced at his friend. "You know, you look like you're about to run for Mayor instead of preparing for a long day of replacing the boiler in the Swift."

Matthew shrugged. "Well, I figure as second in command of the Davenport Dispatch & Delivery company, I might should look the part," he hesitated, then smirked, "at least for a couple hours before I have to go back to looking like a hired hand. Besides, even sodbusters like to have their boots polished every now and then."

Jed chuckled, tossing the cloth he had just dried his hands with. It landed on top of Matthew's head. "Let's just not get so clean that Phineas doesn't recognize us when he gets here with the new boiler.

By the time the two stepped into the hallway, the bustle of the hotel was already in full swing: chambermaids darting with linens, waiters carrying trays, the faint smell of coffee and baking bread drifting up from the dining room. Whatever the day had in store, it was clear that Windmire Junction was ready for it.

Jedidiah Davenport and Matthew Colton descended the wide staircase into the lobby and made their way to the dining room. The scent of warm rolls and sizzling bacon hit them strong as they stepped foot inside. The morning crowd was already gathered. Businessmen with morning papers spread across their tables, families in traveling clothes, a few miners and cattlemen hunched over steaming mugs.

As soon as the two men entered, the room seemed to ripple with awareness. Heads turned. A couple of men whispered behind their napkins; a woman covered her smile with her gloved hand. Jed caught a quick flash of teeth as someone chuckled openly.

"Any guesses what they're laughing at?" Matthew asked, unamused.

"That photograph must have made the rounds already," Davenport muttered under his breath, jaw tight. He glanced over at a man near the door. He had the Windmire Gazette open wide.

"Front page, just like they promised." Jed

tugged at his collar and forced a grin. "Well, at least we're famous."

"Famous," Matthew replied dryly. "I liked it better when we were unknowns."

They pressed on until they found an empty table near the windows. The laughter dulled but never disappeared, a low hum that seemed to follow them as they sat.

Almost immediately, a waiter in a crisp white apron appeared at their side. He was young, nervous-looking, with a tuft of hair sticking up where he'd combed it wrong. He cleared his throat, not quite meeting their eyes.

"Good morning, gentlemen," he said, voice tight with practiced politeness. "Coffee? Eggs? Bacon? We have fresh bread and fruit as well."

Jedidiah leaned back, pretending not to notice the stares prickling the back of his neck. "All of the above," he said cheerfully. "And throw in a steak."

Matthew gave a short nod. "Same, but two steaks for me."

The waiter's pencil paused mid-scratch. He blinked at Matthew, then quickly bent his head and scribbled the order, nearly dropping his pencil before retreating toward the kitchen.

Jed let out a slow breath, his stomach growling loud enough that a woman at the next table stared at him with a raised brow. He ignored it and glanced at Matthew. "People just aren't used to seeing a couple of famous airship captains spending their Christmas holidays in a place like this."

"Airship captains?" Matthew arched an eyebrow. "Don't you mean two chimney sweeps?"

Jed smirked faintly. "Be quiet, you only have twenty minutes before you have to report to the coal mines."

The two ate in silence for a while. Jedidiah tore through his steak like eating was going out of style. And Matthew, no longer concerned with appearances, dispatched both of his plates in record time.

When the waiter finally returned with the check, Matthew slid a few coins across the table before Jed could reach for his own purse. "This one's on me," he said simply, standing and smoothing his coat.

"Why didn't you tell me you were paying?" Jed replied with a grin, tugging his cap low as they made their way out of the dining room. "I would have ordered two more steaks!"

The cold December air hit them as they stepped into the street. Breath plumed before their faces, and the early morning bustle of Windmire Junction swirled around them. Wagons creaked, horses snorted, merchants called out from carts stacked high with winter produce. Though the air was bitter, there were still no signs of snow in the forecast.

Jed stretched his arms. "Well, now that we've survived breakfast, I'd say it's time to check in on the Swift and..."

"Merry Christmas, Mister!" A young boy with a stack of newspapers came rushing over. "Care to buy a paper?"

Jedidiah could see his and Matthew's picture plain as day.

"Not right now," he politely declined. "Maybe later. I've got to go check on my airship."

"Gosh, Mister," the boy looked disappointed. "Don't you like helping out a kid just trying to raise money for Christmas?"

Before Davenport could reply, two old women standing nearby gasped in disgust.

"Isn't that the big oil tycoon who came to town in that floating ship?" One asked the other.

"And then promptly blew it up, almost burning down half the city!" The other replied.

"I hear he also owns the largest freight company in the country." The first woman added. "Besides a huge ranch with thousands of head of cattle."

"It's only one thousand head..." Jedidiah tried to correct the two ladies.

"You ought to be ashamed of yourself for not buying a paper from a sweet, innocent boy like that."

"Jed," Matthew Colton said dryly, "please buy a

copy before we get tarred, feathered, and run out of town on a rail."

"Fine..." Davenport sighed. "How much?"

"Just one cent..."

"The smallest I have is this silver dollar..." He held the coin out to show the kid. The boy quickly grabbed it before Jed could protest.

"I'll take it!" the paperboy shouted as he quickly kicked him in the shin and took off running.

Matthew nearly doubled over, laughing so hard he could barely breathe. Davenport tried to give chase, but the pain in his leg made it hard for him to run. He managed to hobble just a few feet before he stopped short as a figure came barreling down the street toward them. It was one of the men they'd hired to keep watch over the ship, his coat half-buttoned, his breath coming in sharp clouds. He waved wildly as he closed the distance.

"Mr. Davenport! Mr. Colton!" the guard gasped, clutching at his side. "You'd better come quick. There's—there's something wrong with your airship."

Matthew's eyes narrowed. "Wrong? What do you mean, wrong?"

The man shook his head, still catching his breath. "Strange noises. Clanking, grinding, hissing, and a strange ghostly voice."

Jedidiah immediately forgot about the silver dollar as his thoughts turned to his precious race

"I'll take it!" the paperboy shouted as he quickly kicked him in the shin and took off running.

ship. "The Swift is making all those noises?"

"It is," the guard stammered. "At least, it was when I left. And honest, governor, I heard a voice and it didn't belong to any of my men."

Jedidiah's jaw tightened, the color draining from his face. Matthew had seen that look before—the one Davenport only wore whenever one of his airships was in danger.

Jed shot a quick look at Matthew. "Let's go."

Matthew tugged his coat tighter and nodded. "Right behind you!"

****

The landing field beside the depot was already alive with morning clamor. Locomotives hissed on the nearby tracks, wagons rattled over the cobblestones, and porters shouted as they hauled freight. But under all that, the Swift quietly made its own noise. An uneven clanking and hissing echoed from near the helm of the ship off the wooden walls of the cabin.

Jedidiah and Matthew followed the guard at a quick pace, boots striking the icy ground. The gasbag loomed against the pale sky, its brass fittings dulled in the winter sun and its framework giving the occasional creak, as if restless in the cold. The ship should have been silent save for the movements of the burly men hired to watch it.

As they ascended the loading ramp, the guard hesitated at the bottom, muttering that he wouldn't set foot aboard the ship again until he was sure it wasn't haunted. Davenport and Colton exchanged a knowing glance and pressed on, immediately hearing the noises that had unsettled the watch.

Several clicks, sharp and erratic like Morse code, gave way to a burst of static. Then came the voice, faint and ghostly.

"...Jedidiah? Do you read me? Blast it all, answer if you can!"

Jed froze, his stomach dropping. That wasn't a phantom! It was the crackling distortion of Phineas B. Hargroves.

He was trying to contact them through the wireless communication system that he, Jedidiah Davenport, and the fearless adventurer Myra Wilhelmina Bancroft had developed during the Sky Race.

Matthew eyed him sharply. "Well, unless this ghost was educated at the University of London and knows your name, I'd say that's our kindly old professor."

Jed's jaw tightened. "Which means the Icarus is in broadcasting range!"

Davenport immediately rushed to the helm and picked up the transmitter. He paused to glance back at his childhood friend.

"Just don't let him hear you call him old," Jed

warned with a sly grin.

Matthew merely smiled and shook his head.

"Swift to Icarus!" Jed called out. "Phineas, do you read me?"

"My dear boy," the familiar voice replied. "It's high time you answered me! Send me your coordinates at once! Tom Miller and I have the new boiler, along with all three automatons, ready to carry out the repair work!"

Before Jed could reply, a low hum rolled over the landing field. Men outside the airship turned their heads skyward as the ground seemed to darken.

Matthew squinted toward the pale morning sun. "Jed..." he said slowly, "I think Professor Hargroves is here."

A vast shadow swept across the depot yard, stretching over wagons, railcars, and the gleaming hull of the Swift. The rhythmic thrum of engines grew louder, rattling windows in the station house.

Jedidiah dropped the transmitter and rushed to the rail, craning his neck. High above, emerging from a bank of thin winter clouds, the Icarus descended with stately grace. Its massive airbag glinted in the light, brass fittings flashing as the sunlight caught them, while the familiar wood-stained hull cut through the sky like a leviathan of the air.

The shadow widened across the cobbled yard,

swallowing everything beneath it. Matthew tugged his cap low against the wind whipping up from the descent and grinned. "Well, now that's what I call an entrance."

Jed's heart thudded with relief and anticipation. "And just in time," he murmured.

Moments later, the Icarus descended with a hiss of valves and a groan of straining ropes as it steadied in the breeze. Phineas secured the mooring lines, and within minutes, the proud vessel settled into place a safe distance away from the Swift, its engines winding down to a low, steady rumble.

The gangplank clattered into position, and Professor Phineas B. Hargroves was the first to stride down, his greatcoat flapping about his tall frame. He was still wearing his festive Holiday attire. Tom Miller followed at his side, sleeves already rolled up to the elbows, eager for work.

"Ah, there you are!" Phineas boomed the moment his boots struck the planks of the Swift. "I've half a mind to give each of you a sound thrashing for keeping me shouting into that wireless transmitter for nearly twenty minutes."

"Good to see you too, Professor!" Matthew chuckled.

"A lot of good that invention of ours does us if you don't use it!" The older man continued to rave. "I might as well have been using two tin cans and a string to contact you for all the good it did!"

Jedidiah managed a grin despite his lingering worry. "Well, you've arrived just in time, Professor. Any issues back home?"

Professor Hargroves thought for a moment about the blizzard he had caused in the barn the day before and wisely decided to change the subject.

"My dear boy, let us waste no more of this fine December morning," he stated, already sweeping his gaze over the helm as though cataloging every sound and smell. "Let me get down below and see what kind of damage has been done."

A few hundred feet away, three familiar figures descended from the Icarus: Cogsworth, clicking and whirring as his glowing eyes flickered. Artemis' metal frame gleamed in the light, and Apollo, stout and steady, was carrying the bulk of the new boiler with effortless precision. They clanked down the ramp without hesitation, moving in perfect unison toward the Swift.

Matthew gave a low whistle as the three metal men carried the heavy object like it was nothing. "Well, Jed, it looks like we can just sit back and relax while they do all the work."

Jed nodded, glancing back at the automatons working with mechanical precision. "Let's just hope they can get it patched up in time for us to be home for Christmas."

Just as Davenport and Colton were about to follow Phineas and Tom down below, a rising clamor from the street pulled their attention. A crowd had formed near the edge of town, voices urgent, feet pounding. Jed frowned and hurried down the ramp. Everyone appeared to be rushing toward the outskirts of town.

"What's going on?" Jedidiah demanded as he pushed his way through the throng of people.

"It's the orphanage!" a man shouted. "The bank's foreclosed on it—they're auctioning everything off!"

CHAPTER VIII

The Foreclosure

The Milford Creek orphanage sat on the far side of Windmire Junction, spread across several acres of prime land. Its windows were glowing softly, a wreath proudly hanging on the front door, and the great fir tree out front standing tall and decorated festively, the wind tugging at its ribbons. Gifts had not yet begun to gather beneath it, but every child in the orphanage knew that by Christmas morning, the space beneath its branches would be filled with wrapped treasures—left in secret by dozens of people from miles around who still remembered the magic of giving.

But this particular morning, the ground in front of the orphanage was not filled with laughter or carols. It was crowded—a swelling sea of townspeople pressed in around the iron fence, some out of curiosity, some out of concern. At the front steps, a bank representative in a long gray coat stood with a clipboard, barking orders to a pair of porters who were tagging furniture.

Rocking chairs. Toy chests. Bedframes.

On the ground next to the steps, a cluster of children stood shoulder to shoulder, silent and wide-eyed. Their coats were thin, some still in slippers or mismatched boots, the older ones pulling the younger ones close as the cold bit at their cheeks. A little girl clutched a ragged stuffed rabbit to her chest. Nearby, the matron—a tall woman with silver-streaked hair pulled into a tight bun—stood stiffly, arms crossed, jaw clenched. Her eyes followed each piece of furniture as it was carried past, her face set like stone, but her hands trembled. Her two assistants and the cook also stood nearby, wondering what they were going to do next.

"Lot twelve, oak nightstand. Lot thirteen, handmade quilt. Lot fourteen..." A man made check marks on inventory sheets.

Jedidiah Davenport pushed through the crowd, his boots striking the frozen dirt, Matthew Colton right on his heels. The townspeople stepped back as they saw him coming, recognizing his look of determination and the fire in his eyes.

"*Sizzling steam pipes!*" he exclaimed. "What's going on here? Have you all lost your mind?"

A weaselly voice answered, thin and nasal. "Foreclosure, Mr. Davenport. The orphanage has defaulted on its mortgage. The property and everything in it now belong to the bank."

Jed spun to face the source. Mr. Templeton, the local bank officer, adjusted his spectacles and lifted his clipboard like a shield. "The paperwork has already been filed. The auction will begin promptly at 12 o'clock today."

As if on cue, from somewhere in town, the clock tower struck nine, each deep toll was a grim reminder of how little time remained.

Matthew stepped up beside Jed, his voice cold and icy. "You're throwing orphans into the street five days before Christmas?"

Templeton sniffed. "The children will be relocated to other facilities. The bank bears no ill will, of course. Just business."

A sharp crack rang out as Jed's fist struck the inventory sheets, knocking them clean from the man's grasp. The porters froze. The crowd gasped. Even the orphans, gathered wide-eyed on the porch, stared in silence.

"I'll pay the debt," Jed said evenly. "Whatever's owed, I'll cover it."

Templeton bent down, retrieving the scattered papers with a trembling hand. "I'm afraid that's not possible."

"Why not?" Jed snapped.

"Now that the papers have been filed and the proceedings have begun, I can't stop them. Even if I wanted to, I don't have the authority to halt the auction."

Matthew's eyes narrowed. "We'll see about that!" The dark-haired young man advanced threateningly toward the banker.

Templeton gulped and took a step back.

"Gentlemen, please!" he pleaded. "Let's be reasonable."

Before either Jedidiah or Matthew could say another word, a new voice cut across the tension.

"Just one minute, Templeton!" Mayor Silas T. Windmire announced, as he stepped through the crowd, hands clasped behind his back, coat immaculate, mustache perfectly waxed. He was followed by two reporters and a photographer.

All heads turned.

"About time you got here!" Jed's jaw clenched. "Do you know what's going on?"

"Just found out and I've come to stop it," Windmire said smoothly. "But with the law, not fisticuffs." His eyes flicked toward Matthew, then to the banker. "I happen to know there's a buyer lined up for this property who is ready to pay far more than it's worth. I also happen to know that this property still belongs to the children until the 24th. You can't legally evict them or auction off their belongings until then. And if the benefit dinner I've planned for tomorrow evening goes as planned, you won't be able to do then or ever!"

"But... but..." Templeton began to stammer. "I was just following orders..."

"Never mind whatever orders you were following!" Silas T. Windmire interrupted the weaselly-looking man. "You're following my orders now! Return these belongings to the children and leave the premises post haste!"

"But..." The banker dropped his clipboard dejectedly and ordered his hired hands to do as instructed.

"Put it all back," he muttered.

Meanwhile, Mayor Windmire turned, lifting his voice for the crowd. "Everyone, calm down. The crisis has been averted. In the spirit of the season, and out of my own personal fondness for these children, I have taken time out of my busy schedule to suspend this unlawful eviction."

A murmur rippled through the crowd, followed by a round of applause.

Windmire smiled broadly. "I assure you, we will have until Christmas Eve to make sure their debt is paid in full!"

The people cheered—as if he'd rescued them from a fire. One woman dabbed her eyes with a handkerchief.

Windmire tipped his hat and then motioned for a few of the orphans to come and stand around him while the photographer took their picture.

Jed, however, didn't move. His hands were

Windmire tipped his hat and then
motioned for a few of the orphans to come
and stand around him while the photographer
took their picture.

clenched at his sides. His eyes were locked on the mayor.

Matthew leaned in, voice low. "He got here just in time to save the orphanage."

Jed nodded, jaw tight. "And he certainly made sure everyone knew he was the one who saved it."

"You think he did it for publicity?" Matthew asked, glancing at the reporters as they headed back to the news office.

Before Davenport could respond, several small children came rushing over to him and Colton, tugging at their coats and sleeves. Beside themselves with excitement, the children began bombarding them with questions.

"Are you the men who are throwing the Christmas party for us?" one little boy blurted, eyes wide with hope.

Another piped up quickly, clutching at Jedidiah's arm. "And are you really gonna take us for a ride in an honest-to-goodness airship?"

A girl no taller than Jed's waist tilted her head back, her braids swinging. "Ma Tinsley says you own the fastest ship in the world… is it true?"

Jed blinked, caught off guard by the sudden barrage. Their expectant faces tugged at his heart. He opened his mouth, searching for the right words.

Matthew, however, crouched down to their level. "Now hold on, one question at a time." He winked. "First of all, we're not throwing you a Christmas party."

All the children's faces suddenly dropped as they looked at Matthew Colton in disbelief.

Matthew leaned back and flashed a big grin. "We're throwing you the Christmas party to end all Christmas parties! This is going to be the bestest Christmas party anyone's ever had!"

The children breathed a sigh of relief, crowding even closer, eyes shining.

"What about the Swift being the fastest in the world?" The little girl with the swinging braids asked again.

"Well," Jedidiah replied proudly. "It did win first place in an international Sky Race a few months ago."

A little boy tugged on Jed's sleeve. "Did you bring us any presents to put under the tree?" He pointed toward the big fir by the walkway.

Jed glanced over at it but didn't answer at first. Then he smiled.

"I didn't bring them with me, but don't worry, there will be plenty waiting for you at the party."

****

After spending a few more minutes with the children, Jedidiah Davenport and Matthew Colton started making their way back to the landing field.

Frost clung to their coats, and their boots crunched over frozen gravel. Their breath was visible in the cold air, but the sight before them warmed Jed's chest with pride.

The Swift was alive with movement.

Phineas Hargroves stood on the main deck, sleeves rolled up, his long scarf tucked into his vest, barking out instructions like a ship captain during a storm.

Down below, Tom Miller crouched near the boiler housing with a wrench the size of a fencepost, tightening bolts with rhythmic clangs. Sparks flew from Apollo's metal hand as he drove spikes into the wooden planks without the aid of any tool. Cogsworth clambered over the spine of the hull, inspecting rivets and tapping with precise metallic fingers. Artemis was already halfway up the rigging, rerouting steam pipes like an engineer possessed.

Jed whistled low. "Now that's a crew."

Matthew chuckled, raising a hand in greeting. "I think we came back too soon. If we had stayed away longer, you'd be finished by now."

Phineas looked up from a bundle of schematics. "Ah, there you are. I was starting to think you'd taken an early retirement, leaving me behind to handle everything myself."

Jed stepped aboard, patting the railing affectionately. "Well, from the looks of things, you didn't need our help anyway."

"My dear boys," he said with a smirk. "When have I ever needed anyone's assistance?"

Jedidiah and Matthew exchanged a knowing glance before sharing a hearty laugh.

"Boiler's almost installed, without your help." Professor Hargroves continued. "Frame damage wasn't nearly as bad as I feared. We'll have it flight-ready by nightfall or soon after."

Jed stood next to the helm and looked over the pressure gauges. "Good. I want to be able to return home first thing in the morning."

"What about the benefit dinner tomorrow evening?" Matthew asked curiously.

"We'll just have to turn around and come back before it starts. I want to make sure everything is ready for the party." Jedidiah suddenly snapped his fingers as he remembered something he had asked for in the telegram.

"Phineas, did Pat send along those crates of chocolate I asked for?"

"Chocolate!" Matthew's eyes perked. "Say, that reminds me. I ate my last piece last night. I could use another..."

"It's not for you!" Davenport cut his childhood friend off. "It's for the orphans!"

Matthew shrugged his shoulders. "I figured one bar wouldn't hurt."

Professor Hargroves thought for a moment, and

then it suddenly dawned on him. "Bennington didn't send any cases of chocolate." He turned and called down below. "Tom!"

Moments later, the hard-working young man came bounding up the ramp.

"You called me, Professor?"

"Do you know anything about the cases of chocolate that Patrick was supposed to send along with us?"

"Boy, do I ever!" He exclaimed and began recounting the story involving the rotund cook and the confectionery pool he was splashing around in.

"You mean he stacked all the crates next to a hot wood-burning stove?" Phineas asked in utter disbelief.

Tom smirked as he nodded his head.

"The incompetence!" Phineas roared.

"The chocolate!" Matthew blurted—then quickly added, "For the children! The chocolate for the children!"

Tom's grin vanished mid-laugh. "Wait a second…" He remarked as an idea suddenly struck him. He immediately excused himself and rushed down the loading ramp, his boots hammering the deck as he raced into town.

"Where's he going?" Matthew asked.

"No idea," Jed muttered, watching him disappear.

"Perhaps he's following in your footsteps and

taking an early retirement!" Phineas scoffed. "It's fine, however, I can handle it by myself. Think nothing of it."

"We never doubted you," Jed replied just as his eye caught sight of something. A single sheet of paper folded in half and lying on the panel next to the compass.

"What's this?" he asked, picking it up.

Phineas glanced over without much interest. "Telegram. Arrived not long after you left. Haven't had a moment to read it."

Jed unfolded it carefully, eyes scanning the thin, typewritten lines.

His brow furrowed. "We just had another freight wagon held up."

Matthew stiffened. "What?"

Jed showed him the paper. "The replacement supplies I ordered for the orphanage…"

"Same person as before?"

Jed's fist clenched around the telegram. "Two-Gun Kate strikes again!"

CHAPTER IX

The Trail of Two-Gun Kate

"Two-Gun Kate!" Matthew Colton repeated in disgust. "Let's go after her now while the trail is hot!"

"But let's get some backup first," Jedidiah Davenport agreed. He was just as eager to bring the cold-hearted criminal to justice—but not without the aid of local law enforcement.

The sheriff's office sat near the end of Main Street, wedged between the barber shop and an empty feed store. A faded tin star hung above the door, squeaking slightly in the gentle breeze. The windows were dark, and the wooden steps groaned beneath Davenport's boots as he climbed them two at a time.

Colton followed close behind, his brow furrowed. "I hope he hasn't already gathered up a posse and left without us!"

Jed pushed the door open. It creaked loudly,

announcing their arrival.

Inside, the place was a rundown mess.

Lining the walls were old wanted posters that hadn't been updated in nearly two years, and the rack of rifles covered in dust looked like they hadn't been touched or cleaned in months. A half-eaten pie sat on top of a filing cabinet. A spittoon rested right in the middle of the floor.

Behind the once orderly desk—which was now covered in old newspapers and coffee stains—sat a hunched man with whiskers like rusted steel wool and a permanent scowl carved into his face.

"Well, well," the old man muttered, not bothering to stand. "If it ain't the airship farmer and his big city sidekick. What can I do for you boys on this fine, winter day?"

Jed stepped forward. "Two-Gun Kate just hit another one of my freight wagons. We're here to join your posse and go after her!"

"Is that so?" Sheriff Curdle scratched at his sideburns. "Two-Gun Kate, you say? That makes the second hold-up just this week. But don't know nothing about no posse."

"You certainly are calm to just now be learning about this." Matthew blinked. "Or did you already know?"

"I heard tell something about it." The old man scratched his other sideburn just before reaching for his cup of coffee. He took a long, slow sip.

"Don't you think you should round up your deputies and go after them?" Matthew demanded.

"We've got to get those supplies back before Christmas!" Jedidiah added.

"What deputies?" Curdle snorted. "I ain't got no deputies. After he was elected two years ago, the first thing Mayor Windmire did after renaming the town was to fire the old sheriff and his men. He appointed me, but said this town was so law-abiding I didn't need any deputies."

"Well, what about gathering some of the townsfolk for a posse?" Jedidiah suggested.

"I'm not wasting good manpower on a wild goose chase through the hills for some group of kids."

Jed's jaw tightened. "Do you realize how close it is to Christmas and how much those children depend on those supplies?"

"Well, say, you might just have a point." The Sheriff pulled open a drawer. Seconds later, he tossed two deputy badges onto the desk. "How about the two of you go after Two-Gun? If you manage to bring Kate back, you'll be heroes."

"And if we don't bring her back?" Matthew asked suspiciously.

"You'll still be heroes." The old man leaned back and laced his fingers across his belly. "And I'll personally make sure everyone at your memorial knows it!"

Matthew stepped forward. "So you're telling me that you're going to sit here and do nothing while we risk everything?"

Curdle shrugged. "Got my hands full with paperwork. Been meaning to update the wanted posters for months." He picked up a stack that had been accumulating and pointed. "Take this one, for instance. The Clockwork Conqueror. A nasty-looking fellow. Especially with that mask. You boys ever hear tell of him?"

"As a matter of fact," Matthew's impetuous nature was really beginning to show as he was quickly losing the battle to keep his temper in check. "We helped to apprehend him a couple of months ago. He's currently in prison as we speak!"

"Locked up, you say?" The old man looked skeptically at the wanted poster, then said, "Maybe so, but I'll hang on to this until I get official word."

Jed's voice suddenly dropped as he, too, began to lose his temper. "What happened to the old sheriff?"

"Sheriff Granger?" The old man grunted. "Told you, he was fired along with his deputies. Mayor Windmire said we needed fresh leadership."

"Fresh?" Matthew muttered under his breath. "You haven't been fresh for over thirty years."

Jed turned on his heel. "Come on, Matt. We're wasting time. Two-Gun Kate is getting away."

"What about your badges?" Sheriff Curdle

motioned toward the two tin stars.

Jedidiah and Matthew exchanged a knowing glance, then reluctantly reached for them.

"Don't you need to swear us in?" Davenport asked as he pinned his badge on.

"Fine, fine. Raise your right hands." Curdle said, and they obeyed. "You swear to be deputies?"

"We do..." Jed and Matt awkwardly said in unison.

"Okay!" The sheriff put his own hand down. "You're deputies. Now get going!"

Jed paused at the door, hand on the knob. "Don't worry, we'll bring her in. Just don't strain yourself with all that heavy paperwork."

They left the sheriff's office and didn't speak until they reached the hotel, where they rushed up to their room and changed into something more appropriate for riding. While there, Jedidiah glanced out the window.

He caught movement across the street—a curtain falling quickly into place. The same window and the same face from the night before. Someone was definitely keeping tabs on them.

However, they didn't have time to investigate. Their next stop was the landing yard where the Swift and Icarus both gleamed against the frost-bitten hills. As they entered the sleeping quarters of the Swift, Matthew gave a sideways glance.

Jedidiah Davenport was already unlocking a

small cabinet near his bunk. Inside a glass top display case, two paralyzing ray guns lay nestled side by side. Sleek copper-and-brass casings, polished wood grips, and faintly glowing green orbs made them look like relics from some futuristic era. They'd taken them off the gang that held up the train a couple of months back.

"Still working?" Matthew asked, eyes lighting up.

Jed nodded. "I personally tested them on Pat last week."

Matthew's grin widened. "Good. I've been itching to use one again." For a moment, he turned serious. "You sure you want us to do this alone?"

"We don't have time to round up a posse. The longer we wait, the further Two-Gun Kate gets."

"What about the Professor, Tom, and the automatons?"

"The more time they spend away from the ship, the longer the repairs are going to take."

Matthew grabbed one of the weapons and attached it to a custom-fit holster that he strapped to his side. "Then I guess it's just the two of us."

Their next step was the local branch of Davenport's freight company, where Jed acquired two of the swiftest steeds in their stable. They also found out the exact location of the hold-up.

"You sure this is the right move?" Matthew asked, tightening the strap on his saddlebag.

Jed looked out toward the hills. "No. But what other choice do we have?"

With that, they spurred their horses and took off. With the midday sun high above them, they began riding toward the place where Two-Gun Kate had last struck.

****

The spot where the freight wagon had been hit was nestled between two rocky bluffs, the perfect place for an ambush.

Jedidiah dismounted first, boots crunching against the brittle frost. Matthew followed, surveying the area with narrowed eyes.

"Not much left," Matt muttered, stomping the hard, frozen earth. "It's hard to leave tracks on the ground when it's like this."

Jed crouched and began searching the area. A dozen or so feet away, he found faint tracks left by the wagon wheels.

"These look fairly fresh," he said. "Maybe two or three hours old."

"About the time of the hold-up." Matthew scanned the surrounding ridges. "You think she had any help?"

"I don't think so. Nobody has ever reported seeing anyone with her." Jed stated as he walked along the road, leading his horse behind, for the next half of a mile, give or take a few hundred feet. Then he paused, his gaze fixing on a line of faint indentations disappearing into a set of bushes. On closer inspection, he discovered they had been placed there to hide the trail. He immediately moved them to the side, stood, and brushed off his pants.

"Let's see where this takes us," he commanded.

They mounted up again, following the trail at a slow pace. The hills narrowed into a winding path barely wide enough for a wagon. Every rustle of wind through the rocks made Matthew's hand inch closer to his ray gun.

After nearly an hour, the narrow trail widened into a dry creek bed. The wagon tracks continued ahead, weaving between boulders and stunted trees. Faint hoofprints flanked the ruts—riders, maybe two or three, escorting the stolen goods.

"Wherever she's going," Jed said, "she didn't want to be followed."

"Which makes me want to follow even more," Matthew replied.

They pressed forward another half mile before the tracks abruptly vanished.

Jed pulled up on the reins. "Whoa."

Matthew slowed beside him, following Jed's gaze. The narrow trail dipped suddenly into a wide, scooped basin of rock and shale—the remains of a long-abandoned stone quarry. Jagged cliffs walled in the sides like broken teeth, and the brittle air was still, as if the whole place were holding its breath.

"There," Jed said quietly, pointing.

At the quarry's center sat several freight wagons, all unmistakably from his freight line.

"Gosh," Matthew breathed. "So this is her hideout."

They dismounted, tying their horses to a scrubby tree just above the rim. Jed lowered his goggles, which normally rested on the brim of his cap, and adjusted the telescopic lenses.

"She's here," he muttered. "There's an old cabin… I see smoke rising from the chimney."

Matthew tensed. "You sure she's in there?"

"Hard to say from this distance. I can't see through the windows…" he adjusted the lens, frowning.

"Do you think she knows we're up here?" Matthew asked as he began to look through his own goggles.

"Who knows?" Jedidiah focused more on the cabin. "She might even be out scouting another hold-up."

"Only one way to find out," Matthew said, determined, already unfastening the strap on his ray gun holster.

"Wait," Jedidiah put a hand on his friend's shoulder. "Let's not go blindly charging in. This could be a setup."

As he said this, Two-Gun Kate stepped out of her cabin. She cut an imposing figure in her long brown duster, the hem brushing the tops of her boots as she moved. A corseted vest hugged her frame, the brass buckles gleaming faintly in the winter sun. Her polished top hat caught the light, a pair of brass goggles perched on its brim, ready for action.

The sharp planes of her face were unmistakable —smooth brown skin, high cheekbones, and eyes that carried the kind of authority that made men hesitate. A lock of dark hair escaped from beneath the hat, brushing against her jaw as the breeze tugged at it. Even at this distance, she radiated control, every step deliberate, every gesture taut with confidence. Her gloved hands rested near two strange, futuristic weapons holstered at her sides.

Her blasters looked far more intimidating than the ray guns Jed and Matt carried.

"Those aren't Colt 45s," Jed whispered.

"No wonder she works alone," Matthew replied.

Suddenly, Kate yawned and, out of boredom, drew one of the weapons and fired it at a large tree. The old oak exploded instantly, showering splinters in every direction. The blast sent both horses they had borrowed into a panic. They began rearing against their reins.

"With weaponry like that," Jedidiah gulped in agreement. "Who needs a gang?"

Two-Gun Kate stepped out of her cabin.
She cut an imposing figure in her
long brown duster, the hem brushing
the tops of her boots as she moved.

"You still think we can handle her by ourselves?" Matthew asked, concerned. "Shouldn't we get some help?"

"I think you're right," Davenport reluctantly agreed. "Let's ride back into town and round up a posse. We'll start with the workers at the freight office."

Just then, a high-pitched whinny rang out from Two-Gun's stallion. Bandit had caught the scent of their horses.

Kate suddenly turned, as if sensing their presence herself. Her left hand hovered near her other blaster as she scanned the ridge, eyes narrowing while she holstered one weapon and drew the other, the faintest trace of satisfaction curling her lips. She tilted her head, listening for any sound that might echo off the quarry walls.

"Thought you could sneak up on me," she murmured. Her voice carried the lazy confidence of someone who'd been both a hunter and hunted before.

She stepped back beneath the shade of the cabin, eyes fixed on the ridge above. The brass gauges on her blaster flickered as she calmly twisted a dial. The weapon pulsed, its core glowing hotter, brighter.

"Come out, come out, wherever you are," she said softly.

"Stay low," Jed hissed as he started crawling

along the ground toward his horse. It was at this moment that both frightened animals broke free and bolted back the way they came.

The sound of hooves faded into the rocky canyons, leaving only the brittle whisper of wind across the quarry.

Jed and Matthew flattened themselves against the ground, hearts pounding. Neither spoke. Neither moved. They barely breathed, trying to remain silent.

Somewhere below, Two-Gun Kate had to know they were there. Minutes crawled by. Ten. Fifteen. Twenty.

Matthew shifted ever so slightly, adjusting his position behind a large boulder. A gust of wind stirred loose dust across the ridge. Still nothing.

Jed finally leaned close, whispering so low it was almost inaudible.

"You think the coast is clear?"

Matthew hesitated, peering over the edge of the rock. His fingers brushed the cold stone. "Only one way to find out," he breathed.

He started to lift his head just enough to get a better view.

Then came the sound.

A low, electric *whirrrr*—the unmistakable noise of a blaster charging up.

The air itself seemed to tighten, as if holding its breath.

Jed's blood froze.

"Get down!" he hissed, already diving toward his friend.

A searing beam of red light sliced the air where Matthew's head had been a second earlier, vaporizing a jagged chunk of the boulder behind them. Shards of rock sprayed outward in a hot burst.

CHAPTER X

The Big Reveal

The air was thick with smoke and dust from the blast. Jed rolled over, coughing, ears ringing. "You alright?" he rasped.

"Still in one piece," Matthew muttered, wiping grit from his face. "No thanks to her. She almost took me out on my first day as a deputy!"

"I don't think she was trying to hit you." Jed shook his head. "I think it was more of a warning."

They stayed still for a moment longer, hearts pounding, breaths shallow. The distant whistle of wind returned, but there were no follow-up shots.

"She knows where we are," Matthew said finally. "What's keeping her?"

Jed slowly sat up, keeping low behind the boulder. "I'm not sure..."

A long silence followed.

Finally, a voice rang out from the distance, crisp and commanding.

"Mr. Davenport, Mr. Colton, you're a long way from Spoon Fork, aren't you?"

The voice echoed in the stone basin, surprisingly calm.

"She knows who we are!" Jedidiah exchanged a puzzled glance with Matthew.

"Toss your weapons down and come out with your hands where I can see 'em. I'd rather not have to fire a second warning shot. It takes my blasters several minutes to fully recharge." She holstered the one she just fired, its barrel still glowing faintly from the blast, and drew the other.

"What do we do?" Matthew whispered.

Jed exhaled. "We do as she says." He carefully took his ray gun and gently tossed it out just beyond the boulder. Matthew followed his lead and did the same. Fortunately, the glass orbs on each weapon stayed intact.

They stood, slowly, hands raised, and stepped out into view. Kate stood facing them, her stance wide, a blaster still gripped in her hand.

As they came closer, she tilted her head, looking them over with faint amusement.

"I've been expecting you," she said. "Didn't expect you to take quite so long to find me." Glancing at the deputy badges pinned to their vests, she added, "Although I wasn't expecting to see you wearing those."

"Wasn't by choice," Matthew retorted.

"What do you mean you've been expecting us?" Jed kept his tone even. "Were you trying to get my attention with these hold-ups?"

"Don't flatter yourself," she said dryly. "I just know your reputation and figured eventually you and your group of friends would come looking for the missing freight wagons."

"Well, here I am, and I want all the cargo you've taken back!'

"Why would you want to steal food, toys, and other supplies from orphaned kids, anyway?" Matthew demanded.

"Mr. Colton," she said with a laugh. "Do I look like the type that would steal Christmas from children? I assure you that I have zero interest in keeping these things from them."

"Then you won't mind if we load the wagons back up and return them to Windmire Junction?" Jedidiah asked.

Kate gave a slow shrug. "I'm afraid you can't do that, just yet."

Jed narrowed his eyes. "Why not?"

She glanced down at the cabin below them and suggested they continue their conversation inside.

"Why down there?" Matthew asked. "If you're planning to blast us, wouldn't you rather do it out in the open so you don't risk bringing the old shed down on your head?"

"Blast you?" Two-Gun began to laugh again as

she holstered her atomic pistol. "How's that?" Next, she motioned towards their ray guns lying on the ground. "And if it makes you feel better, you can have those back as long as you promise not to freeze me with them."

Jedidiah and Matthew slowly knelt down and retrieved their ray guns from the ground, holstered them carefully, and followed Kate as she turned and began walking down the slope.

The descent into the basin was steep, and the loose shale made the footing treacherous. Kate moved with graceful ease, her coat flaring slightly with each step, her silhouette framed by the hazy midday light filtering through the cliff walls.

Jed kept his voice low as they followed. "You believe any of this?"

"I'm trying to," Matthew muttered. "But if this turns into an ambush, I don't want that sheriff speaking at our memorial!"

When they reached the cabin, Kate pushed the door open without looking back. "Come in. Mind your heads—the roof's low, and the place is even older than it looks."

Inside, the dilapidated shack was just as dim and rustic as ever, lit only by a small lantern and an iron stove crackling in the corner. The scent of burning mesquite filled the air. Several freight containers were stacked high against one wall. A battered desk sat against another wall, papers spread across it in a haphazard sprawl. Maps, schematics, and what looked like coded messages were pinned to a nearby corkboard.

Matthew stepped in and immediately tensed. "This doesn't look like the hideout of an ordinary outlaw. Looks more like the lair of a master villain."

Kate shut the door and turned to them. "Because I'm not an ordinary outlaw."

She moved to the stove and tossed in another log, sparks fluttering upward.

"Then what are you?" Jed asked, keeping his hand near his holster, just in case.

Kate turned, unbuttoning her duster and tossing it over the back of a chair. She removed her hat and placed it on an old shelf, as she let her long hair fall free.

Reaching inside her vest pocket, she produced a worn, leather-bound wallet. With a grand flick of her wrist, she opened it and held it out.

"Special Agent Althea K. Delacroix. Pinkerton Detective Agency."

"You expect us to believe that's really yours?" Matthew asked. "Could've lifted it off a real agent and pasted your picture over it. Don't trust her, Jed. She may still blast us when we least expect it."

"If I wanted to blast you," Kate said evenly, "you would have already been blasted."

Jed's brow furrowed. "She's got a point," he

Reaching inside her vest pocket, she produced
a worn, leather-bound wallet. With a grand flick
of her wrist, she opened it and held it out.

murmured, still studying the badge. It looked authentic. The worn gold emblem bore the unmistakable eye symbol of the Pinkertons.

Matthew blinked. "Wait. So you really are a Pinkerton agent?"

"Been working undercover for the past month," Kate said. "Your freight wagons weren't just hauling supplies and toys. They were transporting something far more dangerous."

Jed's brow furrowed. "What do you mean, more dangerous?"

"Someone's been using your freight company to smuggle futuristic weapons that came up missing from The Clockwork Conqueror's workshop after his recent apprehension."

She raised the lid on one of the crates, revealing a stack of powerful ray guns and atomic rifles.

"Gosh!" Matthew exclaimed.

"Do you have any suspects?" Jed asked.

"Oh, I know exactly who's behind it!" Kate crossed her arms. "I just have to get the proof. In the meantime, I couldn't just let these weapons fall into the wrong hands."

A silence settled over the room as the pieces began to click into place. Jed looked at the maps, the schematics, the trail lines drawn in red.

"Silas T. Windmire…" he said quietly.

"The mayor?" Matthew looked shocked.

"It all makes sense. He got rid of the old sheriff.

He pretends to be on the side of the orphanage but only acts whenever there's press around to make him look like a hero."

Two-Gun gave a grim nod. "You have a keen sense of deduction. I just haven't been able to prove his involvement, *yet*."

Matthew snapped his fingers. "So that's why you couldn't let us take the freight wagons back."

"I'm not trying to ruin anyone's Christmas," Kate said. "But if the two of you showed up with these freight wagons, he might figure things out."

Jed rubbed a hand over his face. "Alright. So what now?"

Kate nodded toward the crates outside. "You can take all the supplies back to a rendezvous point where you can arrange for trusted men to pass them off as a new shipment for the orphanage. I promise I won't interfere in the delivery this time."

"What's the catch?" Matthew asked, suspiciously.

"No catch." Special Agent Delacroix smiled slightly. "You get your supplies back, in time for Christmas, and I don't blow my cover."

"What about the money meant for the mortgage payment?"

The Pinkerton Detective responded by picking up the lock box from the earlier hold-up and handing it over.

Jedidiah looked inside and gasped, "It's only

stacks of bundled newspaper!"

"Exactly!" She replied. "Doesn't it seem odd that the mayor would arrange for large amounts of paper money to be sent by freight wagon instead of having a bank draft sent by courier?"

"That means the money was never even on the wagon!"

"Do you think somebody inside our freight company helped?" Matthew gasped. "I personally hired most of them!"

It was at this moment that Kate's horse Bandit let out a loud whinny, breaking the tension. His hooves struck the frozen ground with quick, sharp beats. The stallion's ears were pricked, nostrils flaring.

Two-Gun Kate straightened, her expression shifting in an instant. She strode to the window, pulling back the curtain just enough to peer out.

Jed instinctively moved closer to the door, but she held up a firm hand. "Stay here, keep quiet, and stay out of sight!"

"What's going on?" Matthew whispered.

"Bandit doesn't spook easily," she murmured, eyes still scanning the ridgeline. "That means someone's coming." The Pinkerton detective placed her hat on her head and stepped briefly through the opening.

Outside, the stallion pawed the ground again, his breath rising in pale clouds.

A moment later, two riders appeared on the far ridge, their silhouettes sharp against the bleached sky. Jed, looking through his telescopic goggles, recognized the cut of their coats and the stiff posture even from a distance.

"Avery and Pierce," Kate said under her breath. "Didn't expect them."

Jed narrowed his eyes. "Mayor Windmire's personal servants?"

"They work for you?" Matthew Colton asked, surprised.

Agent Delacroix turned, giving him a look that was equal parts warning and reassurance. "Yes, but they're not agents. They're..." she searched for the right words "...contractors. They'll do just about anything for the right price. They'll work for anyone who pays them. Windmire included."

Matthew's brows knit together. "So they're fiends for hire?"

"Pretty much," she said simply. "They're doing his bidding while passing me scraps of information. But they don't know who I really am. They think I'm an outlaw who is cutting them in for a piece of the take."

Jed's frown deepened. "And you're trusting them?"

"I'm trusting them to get me evidence," she corrected. "Nothing more." She crossed the room and lifted her hat from the shelf. "They can be useful, but if they see you two here, the game's over. They'll tell Windmire everything."

Matthew glanced at Jed. "So what do we do?"

"You stay out of sight and keep quiet!" Kate said firmly.

"What if they come inside?"

"I won't let them."

She slid her duster back on and checked her blasters. For a moment, she looked every inch the outlaw again, but her eyes held something sharper.

She swung the door open once again, letting a cold gust rush in. "And no matter what you hear," she added without looking back, "don't interfere."

With that, she stepped out, this time pulling the door shut behind her.

Outside, the wind had picked up, rattling through the canyon with a hollow whistle. Agent Delacroix—no, *Two-Gun Kate*—stood tall near the wagon, her eyes fixed on the approaching riders.

Avery and Pierce rode in with casual confidence, though the tension in their shoulders betrayed unease. Their coats were spotless, dust barely clinging to the creases, and their polished boots didn't look like they'd seen much trail. City men, through and through.

"Afternoon, Miss Kate," Avery called as he swung down from his saddle, flashing a toothy smile.

"Fancy finding you all the way out here," added

Pierce, staying atop his horse as his gaze swept the quarry, too quickly to look casual.

Kate didn't move. "You boys lost?"

Avery gave a little laugh. "Not exactly. Heard some chatter in town. Word is, Jedidiah Davenport and his sidekick have been deputized and went out sniffing around for their missing freight."

She let her brow furrow slightly, just enough to sell the performance. "Is that so?"

"Figured you'd want a heads-up," Pierce said, though his eyes were now on her cabin. "Didn't want them sneaking up on you."

"Well, I appreciate the warning," she said, voice cool and steady. "Though I'd prefer it if you two didn't make unnecessary trips out here. If anyone is following, you'll lead them straight to me."

Avery shrugged, adjusting his gloves. "Couldn't take the risk of you getting ambushed"

There was a long beat of silence. Neither man made a move to leave.

Kate's jaw twitched. "Was there more?"

Pierce cleared his throat and shifted in his saddle. "Well, seeing as we might've saved your life…"

"You're expecting payment." Her tone was flat.

"Call it a goodwill bonus," Avery said smoothly. "Just to keep the lines of communication open."

Kate exhaled through her nose, then reached into her pocket and withdrew a small leather pouch.

It jingled faintly.

She tossed them each a few coins. It wasn't a lot, but enough to keep them satisfied.

"Now," Kate said, voice going firm, "ride back the way you came. And if you run into Davenport or his sidekick or anyone else, you never saw me. You never came here."

"Of course," Avery said, tipping his hat. "Pleasure doing business, as always."

Pierce gave a curt nod, and within moments, the two men turned their mounts and disappeared back into the shadows of the canyon.

Kate turned and walked back to the cabin, boots crunching on frost-bitten earth. She was about to open the door when they came riding back up.

"There's one other thing I thought you might like to know." Thomas Avery said slyly. "It's about the benefit dinner tomorrow evening.

The next few words were said in hushed tones, and neither Jedidiah nor Matthew could make them out.

Kate stood still for a moment longer, eyes on the ridge long after they'd gone. Then she opened the door and slipped back inside, her expression unreadable.

Jed and Matthew both stood near the stove, arms crossed, eyes full of questions.

"Well?" Jed asked.

She pulled off her gloves and tossed them on

the desk. "They came to warn me. They said the word's out that the two of you were deputized and sniffing around for clues. They wanted to give me a heads up.

"For a price, of course," Jedidiah added.

"Of course."

"They didn't see us, did they?" Matthew asked.

"No. And they're finally gone." She moved to the crate near the desk and put the lid back over it. "But that's not the important part."

Kate paused, as if weighing how much to tell them.

"They mentioned the mayor is hosting a benefit dinner tomorrow evening," she continued. "It's supposed to be for the orphanage…"

"Yes, we know," Jedidiah replied. "We've been given the displeasure of attending."

"But I bet you don't know what he has planned."

"What's that?" Matthew asked.

Agent Delacroix started smiling as she repeated what she had been told

The wind picked up again, rattling the cabin's shutters, as the three of them began making plans.

CHAPTER XI

The Benefit Dinner

Early the next morning, December 21st, 1881, the aroma of coffee and fried potatoes filled the dining hall of the Windmire Junction Hotel. Morning light filtered through the frost-covered windows, casting golden rectangles across the wood-paneled floor. A small fire crackled in the hearth, doing its best to fight off the bite of winter that clung to the corners of the room.

Jedidiah Davenport sat at a table near the back, hat tipped low over his brow, watching the door. He'd barely touched his plate, and his eggs were going colder by the second. Not to mention the thick slabs of salted pork. Matthew Colton sat across from him, absentmindedly spreading butter over a biscuit.

"They should've been down here by now," Matthew muttered, glancing toward the stairs.

"They were up almost half the night finishing

up," Jed replied. "Let them have a few more minutes of sleep."

Matthew smirked. "Sleep? Who can sleep knowing what we've got planned!"

Jed took a slow sip of his coffee, nodding. "Just remember it's for the children." He paused to look at the newspaper. Christmas Eve was a mere three days away, and still no hint of snow in the weather forecast.

"Guess we can't count on a white Christmas this year." He sighed as he laid the paper to the side.

Moments later, Phineas Hargroves entered the dining room, looking none the worse for wear. Not a speck of dust marred his festive winter attire. The tall red top hat with its gleaming green band, the wide-striped scarf swinging jauntily from his neck. Somehow, even after a long night of work, he looked like he stepped right out of Charles Dickens' classic.

"You look remarkably fresh, Professor." Matthew set his biscuit aside and greeted the latecomer.

"My dear boy," He straightened his posture. "Don't you know that the really intelligent people, such as myself, never allow themselves to look a mess. I use my brains, not my brawn, whenever necessary. I was the supervisor overseeing the repair work. Only creatures of lesser intelligence allow themselves to become covered in filth and walk about looking like mess cats."

About this time, Tom stumbled in behind him, bleary-eyed, hair sticking up in all directions, and one suspender hanging loose from his shoulder. His shirt and pants were both covered in black soot. Jedidiah and Matthew both burst out in fits of laughter.

"Well, that timing was ill-conceived," Phineas admitted as he too started laughing.

"What's so funny?" The brown haired eighteen-year-old demanded.

Jedidiah motioned up and down at his own clothes, then motioned toward Tom.

"Oh," He joined in the laughter. "I suppose the professor already told you what happened."

Phineas suddenly became serious and said, "I don't think we should bore them with that. Let's sit down and order breakfast, shall we!"

"Wait, wait..." Davenport stopped laughing and said, "I've got a feeling I want to hear this."

Phineas quickly tried to change the subject. "You wouldn't believe the things we had to do to get that boiler stabilized. One of the automatons tried to connect the wrong-size pipe to the wrong exhaust port."

"Phineas..." Jedidiah smiled as he said, "What happened to Tom?"

"Well..." He began sheepishly. "I had just picked up the correct size pipe to hand to Artemis when something caught my attention on another part of the ship, so I sharply turned and..."

"...hit me with it, knocking me into the coal bin!" Tom Miller finished the story.

Everyone except Phineas laughed even harder.

"We finished, and that's the most important thing," he said as he took a seat.

Tom yawned as he slumped into the chair next to him. "And all it cost me was a good set of my best clothes."

"After breakfast, you can go pick out a new outfit and charge it to me. In the meantime, order what you want." Jed gestured to the menu.

Phineas raised an eyebrow as he picked up another menu. "Want to tell me how the two of you ended up with those deputy badges?" He asked without even glancing back.

"Okay, but..." Matthew leaned forward, voice low. "You're not going to believe it."

****

After breakfast, Matthew Colton went with Tom Miller to buy a new outfit so he could sign for it and charge it to the freight company. Phineas asked Jed if he had gotten a chance to send the copy of his blueprints to the patent office, as he had asked.

"It completely slipped my mind!" The young entrepreneur admitted. "But don't worry, they're locked up tight in mine and Matthew's suite."

Upon reaching said room, Jedidiah reached into the bureau drawer he had left the papers in and froze. He immediately began searching the dresser from top to bottom. The blueprints were gone!

"My dear boy," Phineas suddenly noticed the look of concern on his young friend's face. "Have you misplaced my diagrams?"

"I didn't misplace them!" Jed looked around the room and for the first time noticed that several things weren't where they had been two days ago. "Someone stole them!"

"Stole them?" Phineas B. Hargroves was visibly taken aback. "Who... when... how..."

"The first night we were here, Matt and I were jumped. Someone dragged us down to the cellar and left us there. Whoever did it must have had full run of the place."

Phineas moved forward, inspecting the door. "No signs of forced entry," he murmured. "Which means whoever took them either had a key—or didn't need one."

"We never locked it. We didn't have time." Jed's jaw tightened. "I should've thought to search the room before now."

"So they were after my diagrams..." Phineas' face went pale, then he suddenly came back to himself. "That's absurd. How would they even know you had them?"

Jed nodded slowly. "I think they were just after whatever they could get their hands on, and it just happened to be your blueprints."

Phineas stood straighter, fingers tightening around the edge of the dresser. "Do you think they'll try to pass them off as their own?"

Jed's eyes narrowed. "We'll find out soon enough. If we see people riding around plowing their fields with steam-powered tractors, we'll know for sure."

"Well, at least I have one thing they don't!" Professor Hargroves stated proudly. "I have a working prototype. I can prove it's my design."

"That's reassuring," Davenport remarked as he turned on his heel. "It won't do much good, but I think we should report this to the law."

The older man immediately reached out and tapped the tin badge pinned to his vest, reminding him that he had been deputized.

Jedidiah chuckled and said, "Well, now that you've reported it to the proper authorities, we can move on."

"Tell me again," Professor Hargoves said as he followed Davenport out the door. "What's your plan?"

Jedidiah sighed and began to repeat the details.

****

Later that evening, the Windmire Junction Town Hall had been completely transformed.

Gaslight chandeliers flickered above a crowd of finely dressed guests, casting warm glows across polished oak floors and garlands wrapped in red ribbon. Long buffet tables groaned under the weight of roasted meats, candied yams, and trays of iced gingerbread. A string quartet played softly near the front of the room, where a large banner read:

"HOLIDAY BENEFIT DINNER – In Support of Our Orphaned Youth"

Jedidiah adjusted the collar of his jacket—borrowed from a mannequin standing in a tailor's shop window earlier that morning—and cast a glance toward the back wall, where Tom stood pretending to be a bored server. Matthew, meanwhile, was making small talk with a pair of city bankers by the punch bowl, keeping an ear out for anything useful. Phineas, in full eccentric formalwear (the very same outfit he had worn to a masquerade ball in Detroit a couple of months ago), was inspecting the mechanical stage curtain with barely contained outrage.

Jed took a deep breath and exhaled slowly. "Alright," he quietly muttered to himself under his breath. "Showtime."

He scanned the building again, slower this time, looking not for faces but for mannerisms. That's when Mayor Silas T. Windmire entered the room, flanked by reporters and photographers from all over. After a few photos had been taken, the Mayor approached Davenport.

"I say, this is going far better than planned!" He announced. "We've almost raised enough money to pay off the entire mortgage, and only half the guests have arrived."

"That is good news!" Jedidiah exclaimed. "Looks like the Milford Creek Orphanage will be around for many more years to come."

"Milford Creek..." The mayor made an odd face. "Doesn't really have that great of a ring to it, does it? I think I'll talk to the matron about changing the name to something more fitting for the town."

"Windmire Junction Orphanage?" Jedidiah asked sarcastically.

"Glad to see we're on the same page!" He patted Davenport on the shoulder as he started walking away. "If you'll excuse me, we actually have a last-minute surprise dignitary attending the event."

"Anyone I know?" Jed asked as he took a cup of punch from a serving tray as Tom passed by.

"I highly doubt you move in her social circles, but perhaps you've at least heard her name,

Baroness Evelina Frost."

Jedidiah nearly choked on his punch over hearing the name. Baroness Frost, head of the *Secret Order of the Clockwork Octopus*, here in Windmire Junction. The last Jedidiah had heard, she was in Paris scouting new recruits and trying to decide what to do with the Aetherwind, Lady Seraphina Blackwood's airship.

"Come along, I'll introduce you!" Windmire motioned grandly for Jed to follow him.

"You know her?" Davenport asked, surprised.

"I know all the important people." The mayor bragged.

The Baroness stood casually near the far side of the room, close to the massive fireplace, dressed in a navy-blue evening gown with silver trim and a delicate black lace veil pulled low across her face. Her dark hair had been pinned up into a neat twist, her makeup refined just enough to soften her sharp features.

Jed leaned slightly to the side to get a better look. His eyes widened briefly as she lifted her veil just enough to smile at him. After a brief greeting, he excused himself and walked across the room.

"Matt," he murmured as Colton passed by with a cup of punch, "don't make it obvious, but look to the left of the hearth. Veiled woman in blue."

Matthew followed the direction with his eyes and blinked. "Is that…?"

"Yep."

"Gosh," Matthew said under his breath. "This is going to be an exciting evening!"

Before they could continue their conversation, more people started coming in, and the noise level of the room began to rise. Eventually, everyone was led to tables where they were asked to take a seat.

Minutes later, they were being served a lavish holiday feast fit for a king and the mayor's ego. Roasted goose with apple stuffing took center stage, surrounded by heaping bowls of mashed potatoes, buttered turnips, and spiced red cabbage. Steaming baskets of golden cornbread and crusty sourdough rolls were passed along with whipped butter molded into festive shapes—stars, bells, and holly leaves.

Mulled cider and hot spiced wine were poured freely, their aroma mingling with hints of cinnamon, cloves, and pine from the garlands overhead.

Dessert followed swiftly: sugar cookies in holiday shapes, mincemeat pies dusted with powdered sugar, and the pièce de résistance—a grand Christmas plum pudding, soaked in brandy and brought out aflame to polite applause. A few children, seated with the matron and staff near the side tables, gasped in awe at the fire-dancing dessert.

Phineas Hargroves sniffed approvingly.

"Nothing rounds off a holiday meal better than a flaming dish of plum pudding," he declared.

Matthew leaned in close to Jedidiah and nervously whispered, "Is it supposed to be on fire?"

"I don't know," Davenport muttered back. "But nobody else seems to be concerned, so just act natural."

Once the flame had died out, it was sliced and served.

Jedidiah took a slow bite, chewing thoughtfully. "Hard to believe this dinner is for charity," he muttered to Matt. "Feels more like the mayor's personal coronation."

"Give it a few minutes," Matthew said. "He'll find a way to make it about himself."

As the last of the dessert plates were being cleared, several staff dimmed the gas lights slightly and the string quartet struck a warm, triumphant chord.

Mayor Silas T. Windmire rose from the head table, one hand holding a polished cherrywood cash box, the other raised for attention. Thomas Avery and Mr. Pierce stood just behind him— flanking him like loyal hounds—each with a practiced expression of solemn dignity.

"Ladies and gentlemen of Windmire Junction," the mayor began, his voice full of celebratory grandeur, "what a spectacular evening this has been!"

A smattering of applause followed, quickly building to a full round. Windmire soaked it in before continuing.

"It is my distinct pleasure to announce that, thanks to your extraordinary generosity, not only have we raised the full amount needed to pay off the entire mortgage on the Windmire Junction Orphanage..." he paused, then gave a tight smile, "...I mean the Milford Creek Orphanage..."

There were a few polite chuckles.

"...we've also raised enough to hire two additional staff, provide modest raises to the current ones, begin some much-needed renovations on the premises, including a new coal-burning heating system. All small things, yes, but essential."

A smattering of applause again.

"Let it never be said," Windmire continued, placing a hand dramatically over his chest, "that Windmire Junction or your beloved mayor turns a blind eye to those in need."

Jedidiah raised an eyebrow at Matthew, who gave the faintest eye-roll in return.

"And of course," the mayor added, lifting the cash box slightly higher, "we'll ensure that every cent is properly managed. As mayor, I consider it my personal duty to see that every child in this town is given the opportunity to thrive."

He smiled widely, white teeth flashing.

"And this..." he spread his arms, looking around

the richly decorated hall, "...this is only the beginning. With the right investments in the future, new opportunities are just over the horizon. Our little town is ready for its next great leap forward. Growth. Prosperity. Progress."

Matt muttered under his breath, "Jed, why do I actually hear *Yankee Doodle* playing in the background?"

"That's because the string quartet just put away their violins and pulled out fifes and drums."

Matthew laughed, thinking he was joking until he looked over and saw the musicians really playing the just-mentioned instruments. "*Guess some people will do anything for money.*" He remarked to himself.

Windmire quietened everyone down again as he raised his glass high for a toast.

"To Windmire Junction," he declared. "To community, to progress... and if I may be so bold... to leadership that knows where it's headed."

"A toast to this speech finally coming to an end," Matthew whispered sarcastically.

Glasses clinked. Applause swelled. The string quartet resumed, sweeping the moment into a golden haze of music and candlelight.

But behind the pleasantries and the polished speeches, Jed's eyes stayed locked on a man in the corner of the room wearing what looked like a fake beard and dark-tinted glasses. He sat there silently watching the whole thing. Something about him seemed out of place.

Mayor Windmire gently tapped the side of the cherrywood box, the metal latch glinting in the lamplight. "This, dear friends, will be placed securely in my personal office safe until the bank opens in the morning. I'm sure we can all agree that after tonight's generosity, we wouldn't want to risk it falling into the wrong hands."

He gave a smug smile, one that practically oozed "trust me."

The audience chuckled politely. Several nodded in approval. A few clapped.

Jedidiah exchanged a knowing glance with Matthew. "You'd think he personally donated all the money himself."

"He's definitely taking all the credit himself," Matthew muttered.

Silas T. Windmire turned and nodded to Thomas Avery and Mr. Pierce, who immediately followed him. Together, they exited through a side door that led to his private office, the ornate cherrywood box cradled in the mayor's arms like a newborn baby.

The party resumed. Music picked back up. Plates were cleared, and fresh cider was poured. For a moment, all was warm and golden once again.

Until—

BAM!

A sharp gunshot tore through the lull of the string quartet.

BAM-BAM!

A second and third followed in rapid succession, coming from the direction of the mayor's office.

Gasps erupted. Chairs scraped back. Several women shrieked as the crowd surged in confusion.

People started running toward the exits—some ducking low, clutching their hats. The string quartet stopped cold, and a serving tray hit the ground with a crash.

Jedidiah was already moving.

"Let's go!" he shouted.

Matthew and Phineas were on his heels. Tom athletically leapt over the buffet table and followed, unfastening the server's apron as he ran.

They sprinted down the hallway and skidded around the corner just as the office door flew open.

Mayor Windmire stumbled out, his hair mussed up and his clothes askew.

"She took it!" he gasped.

"Who took what?"

"Two-Gun Kate!" He exclaimed. "She was waiting for us. She grabbed the money box, fired several warning shots into the floor, broke the window, and leaped through!"

Jed's eyes narrowed. "She didn't hit you?"

"No." Windmire cried. "Fortunately, she didn't

fire directly at me. However, just before she started shooting, Avery tried to stop her—she briefly knocked him unconscious!"

As if on cue, Thomas Avery staggered into view behind Windmire, holding the side of his head.

"Where's Pierce?" Matthew demanded.

"Here I am!" He too entered the room where everyone could see him.

Just then, Baroness Evelina Frost stepped up beside Professor Hargroves.

"Oh my!" She sounded quite disturbed. "You mean to say that villain I've heard so much about was here? Are you sure it was her?"

Windmire straightened slightly, wincing as he began to respond.

"She was dressed just like she was described by all of the men she held up," he insisted. "Brown leather top hat, brass goggles, dark scarf—she moved like lightning. I've never seen anyone draw a weapon as fast as she did."

Baroness Frost stepped closer, placing a gloved hand over her heart as if to steady it. "How dreadful. I do hope she's caught."

"You said she leapt through a window?" Jed asked Windmire, crossing over to the open door.

"Yes, east window. Shattered the glass clean through."

"Odd that we heard the shots but not the sound of glass breaking..." Davenport remarked as he stepped inside. Matthew followed without a word. Phineas lingered only a moment, tipped his hat to the Baroness, and slipped in after them.

The mayor hesitated in the hallway but made no move to enter. "I refuse to step one foot back in there until the sheriff arrives."

Windmire turned to Avery and Pierce, instructing them to go fetch him. They nodded and headed down the hall, unaware that the bearded man with dark glasses was following along behind them.

Jedidiah, Matthew, and Phineas looked around the room, but something seemed off. It was too clean. They saw the bullet holes in the floor and the broken glass under the window.

However, everything else was intact with no sign of any struggle. The mayor's desk was immaculate. Books still sat in their places on the shelf. The safe looked untouched. The grandfather clock in the corner was ticking away as normal.

Matthew leaned out the window, looking down at the ground.

"No glass outside," he said quietly. Calling out loud to the mayor in the hallway, he asked, "You said she broke the window before leaping through it?"

Silas T. Windmire began to grow nervous as if trying to think of the right words. He glanced at the Baroness and then the others who had gathered around. "I... I... believe that's what I said..." He stammered.

"This wasn't a robbery," Jed said flatly.

Phineas nodded. "It was a performance."

Matthew stood. "Everything seems just a bit too perfect. Everything except one thing. If she had broken the glass from inside the room, the shards wouldn't be in here. They would be out there."

"Well, now let me think," Windmire pulled out a handkerchief and began wiping the sweat off his brow. "Maybe she broke the window to get into the room... Yes! That's it!" He suddenly spoke with more confidence. "She broke into the room, not out. I just got a bit confused with all the excitement."

"I think we're looking at a staged heist," Jed said as he pulled open every drawer in the Mayor's desk, looking for the money. He didn't find the box, but he did find a revolver that smelled of gunsmoke from being recently used. He emptied the shells on the desk, noting that three of them had been fired.

Phineas adjusted his cravat. "I suppose Two-Gun Kate left that behind before she jumped out the window."

"Yes, that's exactly what she did." The mayor turned sharply. "I told you—this is a matter for the authorities, now stop messing with evidence. Maybe since Davenport and Colton are wearing deputy badges, they should form a posse and go after that female outlaw before she gets away."

Suddenly, Baroness Frost cleared her throat as she remarked, "I don't think Two-Gun Kate had anything to do with this."

Windmire's eyes flicked toward her in panic. "Why would you say that?"

The Baroness replied by removing her veil completely and slipping her dress over her head to reveal her outlaw clothes. "Because she's standing right here."

"Baroness Frost is Two-Gun Kate!" The Mayor gasped.

"*Sizzling steam pipes!*" Jedidiah spoke up. "The real Baroness is thousands of miles from here. If you actually knew her like you claimed you did, you would have known this wasn't her!"

Windmire's jaw flexed. "Are you suggesting I staged this whole thing?"

"I'm not suggesting," Jed said carefully, "I'm straight out saying it. You staged everything!"

Two-Gun Kate reached into her pocket and pulled out her credentials, revealing her true identity as Special Agent Althea K. Delacroix.

"I suggest you open that safe and hand the money over now." She demanded with authority.

"The safe?" Windmire asked, slightly relieved. "You think I hid it in... gladly!" He walked over and began turning the tumblers. Moments later, he opened the door, revealing an empty vault.

"Where could it..." Jedidiah suddenly snapped his fingers as the thought struck him. "Thomas and Avery!"

"Egads!" Professor Hargroves exclaimed. "They smuggled it out right under our noses!"

"I'm going after them!" Matthew called out.

"Don't bother," the bearded man who had followed them announced as he rejoined the others. "They didn't get far. Got both of them locked up in jail. Neither of them had the money on them, but they did admit to helping Windmill stage the hold-up."

"And just who are you?" Davenport asked, trying not to sound too ungrateful.

The stranger replied by removing his false beard and dark glasses.

"The face at the window!" Jedidiah exclaimed.

Suddenly, Mayor Windmire gasped as he said, "Sheriff Granger!"

"The one you fired when you took office?" Matthew suddenly put the pieces together. "Guess you thought you'd run him out of town for good."

"Well, that wraps almost everything up." Professor Hargroves remarked casually.

"Almost everything," Agent Delacroix replied. "We still don't know where he hid the money."

"And without that, you can't prove anything!" He sneered.

Just then, the grandfather clock in his office

began to strike, announcing the hour to be nine o'clock. Jedidiah turned and looked at it. He hadn't realized it had gotten so late. He pulled out his pocket watch and glanced at it.

"I think your clock is fast. According to my watch, it's only half past eight."

Phineas, Matthew, and Sheriff Granger all examined their timepieces and agreed.

"Guess I've let it get ahead." The mayor began to sweat profusely again.

"You know, when we first met you here in your office, you took great pride in boasting how this clock of yours kept perfect time..." Davenport remarked as he began walking towards it. Mayor Windmire stepped closer, itching to stop him.

"Yeah, you're right, Jed." Matthew Colton moved over next to him. "I remember that too.."

"Gentlemen, wait..." Silas T. Windmire almost panicked as he watched them try to open it, but breathed a sigh of relief when they weren't able to. "See, it's locked up tight. You're just wasting your time."

It was at this point that Tom Miller got tired of standing around in the background, not saying or doing anything. So, he walked up and did the one thing neither Jed nor Matt dared to do. He grabbed the clock and tipped it over, letting it smash against the floor.

The back immediately popped open, and hidden

Tom Miller grabbed the clock and
tipped it over, letting it smash
against the floor.

inside was not only the cherrywood cash box, but also quite a few documents. Phineas' blueprints were among them. However, the most interesting thing was the foreclosure papers on the orphanage, along with a bill of sale made out to a company planning to use the building for a factory. Not to mention, numerous purchase agreements from various known outlaws for the weapons he had already smuggled into Windmire Junction.

Jedidiah bent down and picked up a stack of loose money hidden under Hargrove's blueprints.

"This must be the original donations you claimed my company lost," he surmised.

The mayor didn't respond with words, but the expression on his face spoke volumes.

Tom stepped back, dusting his hands. "I guess this is all the evidence we need!"

Agent Delacroix bent to pick up the papers— and that was when Mayor Windmire moved.

With a sudden burst of desperation, he lunged for the revolver still lying on his desk. Jedidiah started forward, but Althea Delacroix was faster. Her hand flashed to her belt, drawing both of her atomic pistols in one single fluid motion. Jed noticed they were set to their lowest setting.

The room filled with the sharp hum of charging energy.

"Don't even think about it," she warned.

Windmire froze, the color draining from his

face. The revolver slipped from his fingers and hit the floor with a dull clatter.

Althea exhaled, lowering her weapons slightly but keeping her eyes locked on him. "Always the same," she said. "You corrupt types never know when to quit."

She holstered her blasters, reached for her handcuffs, and snapped them on his wrists.

"Silas T. Windmire, you're under arrest for fraud, embezzlement, trafficking illegal weaponry, and a few other charges I'm sure we'll uncover. You're through in this town, Mr. Mayor."

Phineas nodded approvingly. "Well, now that's what I call a delightful way to wrap everything up."

"Delightful?" Matthew scoffed. "You call getting shot at, yelled at, and nearly blown up delightful?"

Phineas straightened his cravat. "My dear boy, I meant the way everything concluded neatly, not necessarily the journey getting there. Besides, for the most part, I managed to make it all the way through this adventure relatively unscathed."

Jedidiah chuckled quietly, shaking his head.

At least there was one thing everyone agreed on —justice had prevailed, and the Milford Creek Orphanage had been saved!

CHAPTER XII

The Winter Storm

The following morning, December 22nd, 1881, the Swift's steam-powered engine purred like new as the airship glided through early morning skies, the vast prairie below blanketed in a fresh layer of frost, but still no sign of snow. On the observation deck, Jedidiah Davenport sat with a tin cup of coffee in his hand and an early edition of the Windmire Junction Gazette spread across his lap.

Next to him, Matthew Colton leaned against a storage crate as he took a bite of a licorice stick.

Jedidiah breathed a sigh of relief as he read the article on the front page. "*A Clockwork Christmas*," he chuckled with a faint smile. "Fitting title, considering the grandfather clock ended up being the key to solving the case."

He glanced at Matthew and continued, tapping the page. "Well, it's official. The town council held a late-night meeting and voted Windmire out of office. Sheriff Granger has been put in his place until proper elections can be held."

Matthew grinned through a mouthful. "Good riddance to bad mustaches."

Jed turned the page. "The meeting was held just hours after the arrest. Looks like public opinion turned fast once all the evidence was discovered and the money was returned. They're also voting to change the name of the town back to Milford Creek and completely remove the stain he left behind."

"Hard to stay loyal when you find out someone has stolen from orphans and is selling high-tech weapons to criminals," Matthew muttered. "What about Two-Gun Kate? Does it mention the offer they made her?"

Jed nodded, skimming. "Agent Delacroix," he corrected with a hint of a smile. "It mentions how she was asked to step in as sheriff, replacing the puppet Windmire installed. She accepted the post, but only temporarily. Says she's committed to her work with the Pinkertons."

"You've got to respect loyalty." Matthew smiled proudly. "Does it mention how she asked us to hang on to our badges in case she ever needs our help again?"

Jed smiled slightly. "I asked her to leave that out," he said, folding the paper neatly and taking another sigh of relief. "The town is finally in good hands."

There was a quiet hum of agreement between them as they looked out over the landscape. Hills rolled gently beneath. As they drew closer to Spoon Fork, the horizon's edge began to look different. It was whiter and more wintry-looking.

"Is that snow?" Jedidiah asked.

That's when the first snowflake drifted down near the railing.

"Gosh," Matthew said, leaping to his feet. "Three days 'til Christmas, and two days before the party. Looks like we're going to have a white Christmas after all!"

Jed turned and walked toward the rear of the ship, staring at the other vessel following close behind, the slower but steadier Icarus. Phineas B. Hargroves stood proudly at the helm, his copper goggles reflecting the sun like twin spotlights, young Tom beside him.

Jed gave a faint smile. "I wonder if they can see the snow from back there?"

It was at this moment that Professor Hargroves' voice began to come over the receiving unit next to the helm.

"Icarus to Swift, can you hear me?"

Davenport immediately picked up the transmitter and replied, "Loud and clear! I'm guessing you know about the snow."

"My dear boy," Phineas replied proudly. "I've known about the snow for days."

"For days?" The young entrepreneur seemed confused. "The paper has been saying there wasn't any snow in the forecast."

"I'm actually responsible for it..."

"JED!" Matthew started shouting, talking over the older man. He pointed towards the horizon.

Within moments, the sky began to blur, and the winds started to pick up. The closer they got to town, the harder the snow came down.

Matthew leaned forward, frowning. "That's not a gentle snow. That's a winter storm!"

Jed sighed, lifted the transmitter, and said, "Tell me again, how are you responsible for this?"

Phineas' voice crackled over the transmitter with far less enthusiasm as he, too, began to see the impending weather.

"Well, before Tom and I left for Windmire Junction, I may have—ahem—rigged my prototype weather machine to the ranch's newly constructed communication tower. To give the *Atmospheric Regulator* a bit more... reach."

Jed stared into the blizzard. "Reach?"

"Oh yes," Phineas went on, oblivious to the tightening edge in Davenport's voice. "I wanted to ensure a light, festive snow for the entire valley. It may have been running nonstop since we left."

Matthew exchanged a knowing glance with Jed. "May have?"

"As in... definitely has..." Phineas' voice quickly

added.

Jed closed his eyes and rubbed the bridge of his nose. "Of course it has."

"Everyone in the valley must be trapped inside with no way to get out!" Matthew exclaimed. "All the roads, trails, and paths must be covered over."

"I can fix this!" Phineas said quickly. "We had a similar issue when I ran a test in the barn. My device simply needs to be turned off."

"Turned off?" Jedidiah scoffed as he tightened his coat around himself. "And you say it's strapped to the communication tower? We can't land anywhere near there. How do you expect us to reach it, by snowshoes?"

"Well, you do have those two sets your parents sent you as an early Christmas present." Professor Hargroves laughed nervously.

Matthew wrapped his scarf around his neck and shivered as Jed asked where he suggested they land two airships in this weather.

"I think the area near the house will be sufficiently safe." Phineas T. Hargroves stated with confidence. "While the two of you are striking out to turn off my machine, I'll be working on a way to clean up the roads."

"How do you plan to do that?" Jedidiah asked, confused.

"Let's just say it's a good thing I finished the prototype of that steam-powered tractor."

About twenty minutes later, the Swift and the Icarus both touched down with more grace than expected, considering the worsening visibility. Snow drifts had piled high around every one of the ranch buildings, swallowing up fence posts and shutting down the oil rigs.

As soon as Jedidiah and Matthew stepped foot off the loading ramp, snow came up to their hips.

Matthew let out a low whistle. "I'm surprised it's not deeper than this, considering how hard it's coming down."

Jed looked around and said, "It probably didn't start out as bad as this. It's probably been gradually worsening over time."

Phineas descended from the Icarus with a gleeful hop, landing in a snowbank with a comical *fwump*. "Don't just stand there!" he called out, brushing himself off. "Get that blasted thing turned off before we start the next ice age!"

"Amazing how he caused this whole disaster and yet he still makes it sound like it will be our fault if we don't stop it?" Matthew remarked as they waded up the front steps of the house.

Once inside, they were greeted by a panicked Pat Bennington and Agatha Porter.

"Land O'Goshen!" The rotund man exclaimed as he spotted both young men. "We were beginning to think we'd never see either of you again!"

"How long has the snowstorm been this bad?"

Jedidiah Davenport asked.

"It started snowing the night the professor and Tom left for Windmire Junction," Agatha spoke up. "It was really nice and gentle to start with, and at first we were thrilled over the prospects of a white Christmas. Then around midnight last night, it just got worse and hasn't let up since!"

"It's that weather machine Hargy built," Pat added. "I just know it! He caused this same type of blizzard inside the barn the day you and Matt left."

"That's what I've heard..."

"You'll never believe how it got turned off," Tom Miller interrupted as he walked in the door, snow clinging to him everywhere.

"You can tell me later," Jed threw up a hand as he raced to the hall closet and pulled out two sets of snowshoes. He handed one to Matthew and strapped the other set to his feet.

"Where are you going?" Pat called after the two daring young men as they raced back into the cold.

Jedidiah turned and pointed dramatically. "Top of the ridge over there. About half a mile north-northwest. Give or take a few snowdrifts."

Pausing for a moment, he turned back to Tom. "I thought you were helping the professor with whatever he has planned for the tractor?"

"I am!" He hastily replied as he started racing up the stairs to Hargrove's bedroom. "He sent me in for his thermal ear muffs."

Jedidiah rolled his eyes. "Of course, because heaven forbid his ears get chilly!"

As Davenport and Colton were trudging out of sight, Tom Miller came blundering back down the stairs with a pair of oversized, fur-lined earmuffs. Despite how warm it was in the house, snow was still clinging to him, especially his sleeves and eyebrows.

"I found them!" he called breathlessly, as he caught up to Professor Hargroves, who, along with the three automatons, was already working on bending a larger copper plate into a curved shape.

"You making a giant shovel?" Tom asked, puzzled.

"My dear boy," Phineas smiled proudly. "You catch on fast!"

He took the earmuffs with a pleased nod and slapped them on.

"Come, Tom!" he announced, sweeping his coat like a stage magician. "While they're shaping the plow. Let's stoke the fire in the tractor and have it ready for Cogsworth and the others to rivet it in place."

Tom helped haul open the doors of a small shed attached to the side of the barn. Artemis had already shoveled snow away from the entrance. The wind slammed the doors hard against the side of the structure. Inside, the steam-powered tractor stood like a sleeping beast. Its bronze boiler was ready to come to life.

Phineas rubbed his gloved hands together eagerly. "All right, Tom. Grab a bucket of coal and let's get it started."

"Started?" Tom gasped. "You mean there's not already a fire smoldering in it? I thought you said we had to stoke it."

"Poor choice of words. It'll just take a little longer than I implied." Phineas shrugged his shoulders.

Around the time Tom Miller began loading fuel into the tractor, Jedidiah Davenport and Matthew Colton were already about halfway up the hillside, headed toward the ridge.

Snow whipped around them in wild, swirling gusts, reducing the world to a blur of white and gray. The ridge loomed above, dark shapes half-hidden behind the curtain of falling snow. Each step Jedidiah Davenport took felt like trudging through wet concrete—the snowshoes helped, but not much.

Matthew Colton was a few steps behind, shoulders hunched, scarf pulled so tight around his mouth he looked like a festive bank robber.

"You sure we're headed in the right direction?" Matthew called over the wind.

Jed grunted, holding his compass out for the other to see. "We should be about halfway there."

Matthew squinted ahead. "You realize I can't

feel my eyebrows."

"And you normally can?"

"You know what I mean! If I die of exposure, I'm never speaking to Phineas again."

Jed paused to catch his breath, planting a broken branch he had been using as a walking stick in the snow. "If we don't make up on that ridge soon, nobody in this valley will ever be speaking to anyone ever again."

Matthew didn't respond. He just rounded his shoulders and pressed on. The incline grew steeper. The drifts deeper.

By the time they reached the treeline near the ridge's top, their coats were crusted in ice and their faces windburned raw. Jed raised a hand to slow them—and then he saw it.

The tower.

It emerged from the blizzard like a ghost ship. A tall metal spire jutting into the sky, rimmed with frost, its crossbeams encased in a slick shell of ice. At the top, clamped to the broadcast antenna, was a round copper dish.

"It's more than likely strapped to the base!" Jedidiah called out as they got closer.

"Great," Matthew huffed. "Which means it's probably buried under only five or six feet of snow!"

Jedidiah squinted through the gale, each snowflake slashing sideways in the wind like tiny shards of glass. He pushed forward, shoving through a thigh-deep drift with a grunt. Upon reaching the base, both of them began to dig with their hands as fast as they could.

Minutes later, the corner of something glinted in what little sunlight there was. It was the unmistakable edge of brass and copper.

"Found it!" Jedidiah shouted.

Matthew waded up beside him, already falling to his knees and digging in the same spot like a dog after a bone. "It's like hunting for a buried Antarctic treasure!"

Slowly, the shape came even more into view. A square, wooden box rimmed with copper tubing, brass valves, and gauges.

A small cast-iron weathervane perched on its domed top, spinning wildly against the wind.

There it was. Phineas' *Atmospheric Regulator*.

The brass gauge on the front vibrated visibly, its needle pinned past the maximum mark. Below it sat a smaller dial labeled *Internal Pressure*, which had also maxed out.

Jed spotted a lever on the back, half-iced over but clearly marked on/off in bold, brass lettering. He reached for it and gave it a solid pull.

Nothing.

He gritted his teeth and yanked again. Still stuck.

Matthew leaned in beside him, brushing snow

off another section of the panel. "Looks like it's been scorched by lightning at some point."

Jed rolled his eyes. "Of course it has!"

He quickly untied one of his snowshoes, raised his leg into the air, and stomped the lever. It moved slightly. Two more rapid strikes of his heel, and it was in the off position.

Davenport and Colton looked around, expecting a loud noise or an explosion or something.

Nothing

They held their breath in anticipation.

Then it happened.

The snow began to slacken.

The wind stopped.

Everything became deadly silent.

Matthew blinked. "Did we just break the sky?"

Jed rose slowly to his feet, brushing sleet from his coat as he looked up at the large metal tower.

The weathervane was slowing down more and more. The rooster perched on top of the arrow became easier to make out.

Above them, the clouds began to thin. The blizzard was fading away.

"I think we did it," Jed said.

They stood in silence for a long moment, remnants of the snow settling gently around them.

Then Matthew let out a sigh and flopped onto his back, limbs spread wide. "Just build an igloo around me, Jed. I'm too tired to make it back to the house."

Jed chuckled as he collapsed next to him in the snow. "I would, but who's going to build one around me?"

****

By the time Jedidiah Davenport and Matthew Colton returned to the ranch, the storm was completely over, but all the effects were still in place. Snow was still waist high, and drifts against the buildings were even higher.

Their footsteps crunched wearily as they approached the front steps of Davenport House—a stately Victorian manor with icicles hanging from the eaves like glass teeth. Smoke curled from the chimneys, promising warmth within.

Pat Bennington stood on the porch, bundled in a coat far too small for him, holding a cup of something steaming. He spotted them coming and raised a hand. "Well, I'll be! You're alive!"

Jedidiah gave a tired wave. "More or less," he replied.

"You turn it off?" Pat asked, eyes wide.

Matthew gave him the high sign. "Jed kicked it so hard, it won't dare come back on!"

Pat laughed, stomping down the steps to meet them. "Land's sake, you look like a pair of frozen snowmen. Get inside before you catch p'new-

Jed chuckled as he collapsed
next to him in the snow.

moan-y!" he said, hitting every syllable like it owed him money. "I've got some fresh hot chocolate on the stove!"

Behind them, a low chugging began to rise— followed by a mechanical *grind-grind-hiss* echoing over the snow like a prehistoric creature waking from slumber.

"Oh! Looks like the Professor's had some success too."

Jed and Matthew didn't turn around right away. They were too busy peeling ice from their scarves.

"Jed... Matt..." The rotund man spoke up, but neither responded.

"Uh… fellas?" Pat said again, this time louder. He took a step back. "You might wanna move... Jed —MATT—LOOK OUT!!"

The two young men turned around, just in time to see a wall of snow being plowed up by Phineas' invention. The entire thing covered them over in a complete avalanche of freezing slush.

Pat yelped and took a step back as snow rolled across the porch like a tidal wave, coating everything in a fine dusting. When it cleared, Jed and Matthew were completely buried up to their necks—eyes blinking, faces slack with disbelief.

Phineas B. Hargroves rumbled by on his steam-powered plow, seated high behind the engine with a pair of brass goggles on his forehead and a scarf trailing behind him like a victory flag. Tom stood on the frame behind him, holding to the back of his seat and grinning like a kid on Christmas morning.

"Marvelous, isn't it!" Phineas shouted to Pat Bennington over the chugging, blissfully unaware of the two heads poking out of the snowbank. "The snowplow works better than expected!"

"Hi, Jed! Hi, Matt!" Tom added as he spotted his two friends. "We're going to dig out the valley. We'll be back when we can!"

Jed spat out a mouthful of snow and glared. "Pat, is that chocolate really hot?"

"Pipin'!"

"How's about just pouring it over me?"

"Sure thing..." Pat turned briefly to do as instructed, then he realized what he was doing.

"Oh!" He exclaimed. "Hang on, I'll go get a pail and a shovel!"

****

Two days later, Christmas Eve finally arrived. It was Saturday, December 24th, 1881. Phineas B. Hargroves stepped back and admired the massive, garland-wrapped rafters of the Davenport barn. Above him, strings of lanterns—each one retrofitted with a colored lens—cast warm hues across the walls, dappling the space in red, green, and gold.

"Pat, to the left. No, your left!" he called,

gesturing wildly toward a settee the rotund man and the matronly housekeeper were wrestling into place.

"I am goin' left!" Pat Bennington huffed, puffing under the weight of the new furniture. "It's this sofa that keeps wanderin' off!"

Agatha Porter dropped her end right where she stood and took a deep breath. "It looks fine right here," she said dryly, reaching up and adjusting the bun on top of her head..

"Just making sure everything's perfect," Phineas said, dusting his hands and stepping forward to fluff a pillow with scientific precision. "We are, after all, expecting VIP guests."

Pat straightened up and looked around. The barn had come a long way. Rugs had been laid down over the dirt floors, newly arrived chairs and settees had been arranged in clusters, and a few long banquet tables waited under the loft, half-draped in a festive red-and-green cloths.

"It's a good thing you got all the roads and trails cleared between the ranch and Spoon Fork," he muttered, wiping his brow. "We might be sitting on the floor tonight."

Agatha hung a few decorations on the tree. "You sure those two cats, Dottie and Panther, are going to stay put up in that hay loft?"

"They gave me their word," Pat assured her.

"Gave you their..." Phineas rolled his eyes.

"Don't start that again."

"Don't worry, Hargy," The rotund man smiled. "They've got plenty of food and water to last them till New Year's. They won't disturb the party!"

"Pat..." Agatha said, looking up. "There are only two cats out here, aren't there?"

"As far as you, Jed, or any of the others know," he chuckled. "How come?"

"I thought I just spotted five sets of eyes staring at me, and one of them looked tiny and pink."

Before the bearded man could respond, the sounds of numerous guests arriving from town began to fill the air. In less than an hour, the barn was halfway full, waiting on the arrival of the orphans and their Matron. Suddenly, the familiar sound of the airship known as the Swift began to fill the air. Minutes later, it landed a couple of hundred feet away from the barn.

"Where's Tom?" Phineas asked, puzzled. "He won't want to miss this!"

"He said he had something to do and he'd join us later with a surprise." Pat Bennington explained.

The barn doors creaked open just as Phineas was adjusting the final lantern. A gust of cold air swept inside—and with it, the sound of boots crunching snow.

Jedidiah Davenport stepped into the glow of the lanterns, his overcoat dusted with frost, followed closely by Matthew Colton... and then a stream of bundled-up children, wide-eyed and beaming.

Gasps and applause erupted from inside.

"The guests of honor have arrived!" Pat shouted, throwing his arms in the air.

Agatha Porter clapped a hand over her mouth, her eyes misting as the orphans stepped in, taking in the transformed barn—flickering lights, polished furniture, glowing stove, and the smell of cinnamon in the air.

"Whoa..." one of the smallest children whispered. "It's beautiful."

Jed knelt beside him and smiled. "It is indeed!"

Music picked up again in the corner where a few townsfolk had brought out instruments. The kids scattered in delighted chaos, warming up by the stove, climbing onto cushions, and sneaking peeks under the eight-foot tree.

Sometime later, just as Jed raised a mug of cider to offer a toast, a loud thump echoed overhead.

Followed by a second.

Then a metallic scraping sound—like boots against tin—and the creak of ropes being strained.

The music stopped. Every eye turned upward.

"...Tell me that was just the wind," Matthew said, narrowing his eyes at the ceiling.

Another bang, this time directly overhead.

Agatha grabbed Pat's arm. "There's something up there!"

Pat blinked. "You don't think it's a burglar, do

you?"

From outside, someone shouted, "HEY!
LITTLE HELP?!"

Everyone rushed out the barn doors just in time
to see Tom Miller clinging to a rope ladder
dangling from the side of an airship. He was
dressed head to toe in a bright green elf costume—
complete with floppy hat, curled shoes, and a wide
grin half-frozen by the wind.

Above him, Jonathan Blake's airship, the
Inspiration, hovered with gentle authority. A
crimson banner hanging over its hull, emblazoned
with the words:

SPECIAL DELIVERY — NORTH POLE
EXPRESS

Tom waved frantically. "Someone wanna grab
me?! The roof is slipperier than it looks!"

On the ship above him, a jolly figure in a red
robe leaned over the railing—Jonathan Blake,
complete with beard, belly, and sack of gifts slung
over his back. He let out a deep, theatrical laugh.

"Merry Christmas!"

A second elf poked his head out of the gondola
—Edwin Bancroft, cheeks red and expression
mildly embarrassed.

Once Santa and his elves were safely on the
ground, Phineas pulled Tom Miller to the side and
asked how he managed to arrange this.

Tom grinned. "Back in Windmire Junction…

when I realized how important the chocolate shipment was, I sent a wire to Edwin and Mr. Bancroft. They were in London visiting Edwin's Aunt Myra. Figured they could pick up a few crates on their way back."

Jonathan, dressed as Old Saint Nick, took center stage. He turned and opened the sack—inside were boxes of chocolates, cookies, candies, and a stack of small presents.

The orphans, already crowding forward, let out a collective cheer.

Jed stared at Tom, shaking his head in disbelief.

"You're unbelievable," he said slowly.

Tom Miller shrugged. "Just doing what any good elf would do in my situation."

Matthew and Jedidiah exchanged a knowing glance, then burst out in hearty laughter.

****

Later that night, on the way back to Windmire Junction, the Swift sailed silently through the sky, gliding over the snow-covered valley. Inside the cabin, the children were bundled in borrowed blankets, huddled near the warm ducts as Phineas carefully monitored the controls. Jed stood at the helm, arms folded across his chest, watching the horizon.

"They're all falling asleep," Matthew said softly,

stepping up beside him. "They must have been exhausted."

Jed smirked. "Well, they did just meet Santa Claus."

Below, the orphanage slowly came into view—a grand Victorian manor wrapped in wreaths and glowing windowlight, its peaked turrets and arched windows dusted with snow. A winding brick path led up to the wide front porch, where evergreen garlands curled around the banisters, and golden light spilled warmly from every window. But it wasn't just the house that caught their attention.

It was the tree.

Out front stood the towering fir, its branches weighed down with carefully placed candles, each one flickering safely in diamond-quilted glass lanterns. Strings of hand-twisted popcorn and paper garlands swayed gently in the breeze. The whole thing glowed against the night like a beacon. But that wasn't all.

Underneath the tree, piled neatly on a blanket, were dozens of gifts. Wrapped parcels in bright paper and ribbon, baskets full of apples, toys carved from wood, knitted scarves, boots, dolls, and more. Even from the air, they could see the colorful tags and curling handwriting.

People from all over had been here. Quietly, and without fanfare.

"My stars…" Phineas murmured, returning his

goggles to the top of his hat.

As they descended, it began to snow again— soft and gentle flakes falling from the sky.

Jed leaned against the railing, marveling at it. He turned to Professor Hargroves, who merely smiled and said, "It wasn't me."

Matthew joined both of them, watching as the orphanage's front door creaked open. A few of the staff who had remained behind stepped out.

And as the Swift touched down, they raised their hats and in unison called out a joyful "Merry Christmas!"

Christmas Morning

Despite returning so late the night before, Jedidiah Davenport woke up bright and early Christmas morning, December 25th, 1881. The smell of Pat Bennington's holiday feast had wafted all the way up to the third floor, where his bedroom was situated.

He blinked a few times as he sat up in bed and glanced over at the frosted windowpanes. A small, gentle snowfall continued to come down from the sky. For the first time since he couldn't remember when, there were no alarms to respond to, no missing artifacts to recover, no corrupt villains to subdue, no fires to put out—literal or otherwise. Just the smell of cinnamon rolls, the faint sound of laughter from down below, and the soft creak of his familiar home expanding in the warmth of the fireplaces.

Still in his union suit and stocking feet, Jed

crossed to the window and pushed it open just a crack. The cold instantly nipped at his face, but he didn't mind. The snow was no longer a threat. It was beautiful. The entire valley, blanketed in a pure, unbroken blanket of white, was breathtaking. Everything sparkled—rooftops, treetops, even the water tower attached to the rear of the house.

Down below, he spotted Tom Miller and Edwin Bancroft already outside, bundled in thick coats and fur-lined hats. They were coming from the stables where they had just taken care of the horses.

Jed chuckled and turned back toward his nightstand, where something caught his eye.

A small wrapped package had been left beside his oil lamp. No tag. No handwriting. Just a neat ribbon and a sprig of cedar tucked beneath the twine. Curious, he sat down and opened it slowly.

Inside were four tickets to a carnival to be held in October of 1882 in Chicago, Illinois. Along with the tickets was a short handwritten note:

Nothing in comparison to the event that will be coming eleven years after this one, but it is highly recommended that you attend.

– Mr. F.

Jed reread the note, trying to recognize the handwriting. "Who is Mr. F., and how did he get into my room? Also, what event are they planning

Still in his union suit and stocking feet,
Jed crossed to the window and
pushed it open just a crack.

for Chicago in 1893?" He mused to himself.

Shrugging his shoulders, Davenport closed the lid, tucked it into his coat pocket, and headed downstairs.

The first floor was already alive with activity. Pat Bennington was waddling between the kitchen and the dining room, humming a tune that may or may not have been "*Jingle Bells.*"

Agatha Porter was wondering why he chose to hum a tune that she personally still considered to be a Thanksgiving melody. However, she didn't question him. She quietly continued setting out trays of sweet rolls while simultaneously trying to prevent Matthew Colton from eating them all before breakfast was officially served.

Inside the parlor, Phineas B. Hargroves was seated in an armchair near the hearth, wearing a velvet smoking jacket and a pair of fur-lined slippers that looked utterly ridiculous—and yet, on him, somehow dignified.

"Merry Christmas!" Phineas called out grandly, raising his teacup as Jed entered. "I trust you slept peacefully knowing the entire valley was enjoying this winter wonderland!"

Jed just shook his head, grinning. "You know, you almost buried the entire county in this winter wonderland."

"My dear boy," the professor replied, waving a hand. "That's entirely beside the point, and besides,

I fixed it, didn't I?"

"You mean *we* fixed it?" Matthew called from the hallway, stepping in with a steaming mug in hand. "You just cleaned up the roads with the plow that you nearly buried us alive with."

"Details," Phineas muttered, taking another sip.

The smell of cinnamon, roasting ham, and pine needles filled the air. The fire popped in the hearth. Outside, the snow gleamed and sparkled like the inside of a storybook.

And for one perfect morning, the world felt at peace.

About this time, Tom Miller and Edwin Bancroft came bounding into the house. "Time to open presents!" They cheerfully announced in unison.

"Father!" Edwin called up the stairs to Jonathan Blake. "Come downstairs before we start opening gifts without you!"

Jonathan Blake descended a moment later, already tying the sash of his robe and muttering something about "at least let me have my coffee first." He looked around the parlor at the assembled crew and gave a small, tired smile. "Merry Christmas, everyone."

"Welcome back. You and Edwin made it just in time!" Agatha said, handing him a steaming mug of cider and motioning toward the tree in the parlor.

It wasn't nearly as tall as the one in the barn, but

it was decorated just as festively in silver tinsel. Underneath were piles of wrapped parcels—all neatly arranged according to Professor Hargroves' standards.

One by one, the room filled with the sounds of laughter and rustling paper.

Pat Bennington received a brand-new derby to replace the bowler he lost a couple of months back.

Matthew unwrapped a brand-new set of spats, from Phineas, and immediately slipped them over his boots like he was putting a crown on his feet.

"I'll be the best-dressed sod buster who ever set foot aboard an airship," he said, lifting his foot theatrically.

Tom Miller and Edwin Bancroft each received a set of their very own telescopic goggles.

"Tom, my dear boy," Phineas spoke up. "You should have had those when you were hanging on to the back of the snowplow."

Jedidiah received a pocket-sized leather journal, embossed with his initials, and a short note written this time in familiar handwriting:

"To chronicle the many adventures we've left to face."

Jed smiled and ran his thumb along the edge of the pages. The first two pages were already filled in. A simple sketch of the Phoenix, his first airship, and one of the Swift, his speediest. They were both drawn with care and precision in ink. It was unmistakably Matthew's work.

He stared at it for a long moment, quiet. Then said only, "Thanks, Matt."

Suddenly, Professor Phineas B. Hargroves stood to his feet and turned to Jedidiah with the air of a theatrical stage performer, then produced a boldly wrapped box from behind the armchair. "For you, my dear boy!"

Jed accepted it with mild suspicion, gently peeling away the ribbon. Inside was a top hat—not just any top hat, but a loud, striped top hat in vivid alternating bands of electric green, cobalt blue, and black. Its brim was wide and slightly curled, the crown a touch exaggerated in height. It looked like something that had been based on a nightmare someone had after thinking about merging a candy shop and a haberdashery.

Jed just blinked at it. "Wow."

"Striking, isn't it?" Phineas beamed. "Imported felt, hand-dyed. Bold. Daring. Undeniably modern. This, my boy, is the future of fashion."

Jed held it up slowly for the others to see. "It's... definitely something."

At that moment, Pat Bennington leaned over for a better look and gasped. "That's the most beautiful hat I've ever seen in my entire life!"

Phineas froze, his confident smile faltering. "It is?"

"I mean, look at it!" Pat went on. "It's got flair!

It's got spunk! If I wore that hat, I'd never take it off again."

The professor's expression had gone strangely neutral. "Well. Hm."

Jed tried the hat on. It listed slightly to the side. He looked like a circus ringleader who had just lost his elephants.

Matthew gave him a long, slow look. "You know... it actually kind of suits you."

Phineas suddenly seemed to reconsider. "...Perhaps it's not too late to return it and get you something less... bold..."

But before he could sink too far into second-guessing, Pat stood and reached into a small bag by the hearth. "Speaking of bold fashion, I almost forgot! Got something for you, Hargy!"

He handed over a long, narrow parcel wrapped in newspaper and tied with kitchen twine.

Phineas opened it to reveal a bright blue tie with a large yellow daisy hand-painted right at the center. The petals curled up like a sunrise. It was charming in that proudly handmade sort of way.

"An old lady down the alley where I got my old derby painted it," Pat said proudly. "She had hands like gnarled tree roots, but the steadiest brush I've ever seen. Thought of you right away."

Phineas held it up uncertainly. "It's… much longer than the cravats I normally wear."

"Don't worry, Hargy. I thought of that. You can

just wear it on the outside of your vest!" Pat encouraged. "That way everyone's sure to notice!"

There was a pause as everyone waited for Phineas' response.

"I do like being noticed," he finally admitted, holding it up to his chest. "And it does have an air of whimsical elegance."

"You'll be the toast of the town wherever you go," Matthew added helpfully.

"My dear boy," Phineas said, lifting his chin proudly. "I already am."

They all laughed as the rest of the presents were passed out. Everyone there had gotten something for everyone else. Among other things, Jedidiah received another brand new pocket watch from his head foreman, Jim Davis, and the rest of the hired hands on the ranch. Unlike his others, this one looked plain but was made of solid copper.

"How many watches do you have now, Jed?" Pat Bennington asked.

"Enough to warrant building a display case and charging admission," he chuckled.

After everyone thought the last gift had been handed out, Agatha pulled out one final package from behind the piano. "I didn't forget you," she said, placing it in the professor's lap. "Though I debated for a while whether I should give it to you or not."

Phineas unwrapped the box eagerly—and inside

was a pair of thick wool socks, stitched with the initials PBH and a note reading: "For the next time you cause a winter storm."

"I shall treasure them always," he declared, as everyone broke into laughter.

And then, just as the chaos was beginning to quiet, Jedidiah Davenport finally brought up the subject of the barn blizzard they had started to tell him about but never finished.

"How did you manage to turn the machine off if you couldn't get close to it?" He asked.

"You'll never believe it..." The older man shook his head.

"Don't tell me it was a black cat wearing a top hat?" Matthew chuckled.

"No," Tom Miller spoke up hesitantly, "but would you believe a little white mouse in a metal suit toting a lightning rod?"

Everyone laughed—except Phineas, who now looked genuinely concerned.

But the laughter didn't stop. It rolled through the parlor like a familiar song, rising with the warmth of the hearth and the scent of cinnamon in the air. Outside, snow continued to fall in gentle, sleepy flurries.

And inside, for just a little while longer, all was calm. All was bright.

****

This holiday standalone adventure wasn't the end of Jedidiah Davenport's journey. Be sure to check out The Mechanical Rebellion: A Jedidiah Davenport Adventure, the fourth official book in the series.

As humanity stands on the brink of a war like no other, Jedidiah must rally his allies to face the rising tide of automatons gone rogue. Can they restore peace before it's too late? What truths lie hidden within the gears of rebellion? Join us for the next thrilling chapter of Jedidiah's saga and find out!

And for those wondering about Matthew and Tom's comments about the top-hat-wearing black cat and the white mouse in a metal suit…

Don't miss the enchanting spin-off series:

Steampunk Velvet: A Victorian Cat and Her Amazing Adventures

Velvet the cat may be small, but her wit is sharp, her hat is impeccable, and her adventures are anything but ordinary. From tangled alleyways to strange laboratories, she and her unlikely companions face curious dangers, mechanical mischief, and more than one connection to Jedidiah's ever-expanding world.

Current titles in the
Jedidiah Davenport Adventure Series

Holiday Specials

Current titles in the
Steampunk Velvet Adventure Series